AUG '06

Mightier
Than the Sword

Mightier
Than the Sword

WORLD FOLKTALES
FOR STRONG BOYS

Collected and told by **Jane Yolen**

With illustrations by **Raul Colón**

SILVER WHISTLE • HARCOURT, INC.

Orlando   Austin   New York   San Diego   Toronto   London

Requests for permission to make copies of any part of the work should be
mailed to the following address: Permissions Department, Harcourt, Inc.,
6277 Sea Harbor Drive, Orlando, Florida 32887-6777.

www.HarcourtBooks.com

Silver Whistle is a trademark of Harcourt, Inc., registered
in the United States of America and/or other jurisdictions.

Library of Congress Cataloging-in-Publication Data
Yolen, Jane.
Mightier than the sword: world folktales for strong boys/Jane Yolen;
illustrated by Raul Colón.
p.   cm.
"Silver Whistle."
Summary: A collection of folktales from around the world
that demonstrate the triumph of brains over brawn.
1. Tales.   [1. Folklore.]   I. Colón, Raul, ill.   II. Title.
PZ8.1.Y815Mi   2003
398.2—dc21   2002009886
ISBN 0-15-216391-3

Text set in Meridien Roman
Designed by Kaelin Chappell

E   G   H   F

Manufactured in China

Contents

An Open Letter to My Sons and Grandson

This book is for you. It is for you because this book did not exist when I was growing up.

This book is for you because for the longest time boys didn't know that being a hero was more than whomping and stomping the bad guy. They didn't understand that brains trump brawn almost every time; that being smart makes the battle shorter, the kingdom nearer, the victory brighter, and the triumph greater.

This book is for you because *hero* is a word for winner, not whipper; for smarty, not smarty-pants; for holding on, not holding back. *Hero* is about being clever, learning from your mistakes, being kind and compassionate, and finding good friends. Picking up a sword doesn't make you a hero—sticking to your word does.

This book is for you because these stories have always been around, though the muscle-bounders too often have taken the headlines away. And this book is for you because you may not have the time or energy to try to find these stories by looking through the hundreds of hero stories that always end—like so many *Star Trek* episodes—with a battle or a brawl.

This book is for you because the stories have always been there, not only in folk traditions but in history as well, if you know where to look.

Think of heroes like Mahatma Gandhi and Martin Luther King Jr., who taught us that one can win simply by refusing to bow down to power. Gandhi helped free India from British rule by showing the British that he would fight by resisting passively. Martin Luther King Jr. did something similar for African Americans, all the while reminding Americans that we share a common dream.

Think of heroes like Charles Darwin, who changed the way we think about the world simply through the power of his mind. As did Sir Isaac Newton and Albert Einstein, who made greater differences in the world than Attila or Napoleon or Hitler, men who caused the deaths of millions with their egotistic and power-hungry posturings.

Think of the quiet heroes like John Chapman, known familiarly as Johnny Appleseed, who changed the face of the western United States by planting apple orchards from Pennsylvania to Illinois, to help pioneer families as they traveled to new homes. Like Meriwether Lewis and William Clark, who undertook an eight-thousand-mile expedition from 1804 to 1806, to map the western part of the United States. Or Jacques Cousteau, who popularized the mysteries and beauties of the sea, and warned about dangers to the delicate balance of the ocean's ecosystem. Or early astronauts like Neil Armstrong and Buzz Aldrin, who risked life and limb to set foot on the moon. Or the firefighters, police, and paramedics who, without regard for themselves, ran to help others on September 11.

This book is for you not because I think one should *never* have to fight, but because I think the true heroes are the ones who solve their problems—and the problems of the world—without ever having to resort to force. The tongue is mightier than the sword. As is the pen.

This book is for you because I want you to become *that* kind of hero.

Your loving

Nana

Mightier
Than the Sword

CHINA

The Magic Brocade

A hero's knees do not buckle at the first problem

Many years ago, in a small village in China, lived a weaver and her three sons: Zhu, Shen, and the youngest, Wang Xing.

Now the weaver was a widow and had to support her family by herself. However, she was very skilled—especially at weaving brocade with silver, gold, and silk threads running through. It was said that the animals and birds in her brocades were so lifelike, they looked as if they were ready to leap off the cloth and run into the woods. So, by selling all that she wove, the weaver and her sons lived comfortably, though they were far from rich.

One day, as the widow went through the market carrying her latest weavings, her eye fell upon a beautiful painting. It was of an exquisite white house sitting in the middle of a glorious garden. Among the bushes fluttered red birds, the likes of which she had never seen. A silver river coiled around house and garden, and beyond the river was a forest full of green and gold trees.

"Ah!" she sighed. "I must have this picture." She traded all of her weavings for it and took the picture home.

Placing the picture on the table, she sat down and stared at it, sighing again and again. When her sons came in from the fields, she showed the picture to them. "How I wish we could live in such a place."

Zhu and Shen laughed. "Mother, it is only a painting."

But Wang Xing put his arms about her shoulders. "Why not weave a copy of the picture in a piece of cloth?" he said. "That will be almost like living in it."

"Thank you, my youngest son," said the weaver. Without even cooking the evening meal, she went to her loom and began to work.

From then on, she worked morning, noon, and night on the weaving, sleeping little and eating less.

Zhu and Shen soon grew annoyed. "She is making nothing for the market," they told each other. "There is no food on the table. There are no clean clothes."

Wang Xing took them aside. "Do not trouble our mother, brothers. If you chop wood and sell it, I will do all of her chores. That way Mother can keep her dream. For has she not supported us all these years?"

"Pah!" said Zhu.

"Hah!" said Shen.

But they did as Wang Xing had asked, because he had shamed them.

Weeks passed and still the weaver worked only on the one brocade. Now the older brothers grew tired of chopping wood and hauling it to the market for sale.

Once again, they went to complain to their mother. Once again, Wang Xing stopped them.

"Let me do the chopping and the selling," Wang Xing said. "Let me do all the household chores. Just comfort Mother, and bring her tea."

A year passed. Tears from the weaver's eyes dropped onto the brocade, making the river in the brocade shimmer.

Another year passed. Blood from her pricked fingers dropped onto the bright birds in the brocade, making them shine.

2

Finally, the third year came and nearly went, and the brocade was finished at last. The white house sat proudly in the middle of the garden. Among the colorful bushes fluttered shining red birds. The coiled silver river shimmered, and behind the river stood a forest full of green and gold trees. And something new—sheep and cattle and goats grazed contentedly in the fields. All this the widow had woven into the brocade. It was a masterpiece.

She took the brocade outside to look at it in the sun, for her eyes had grown so dim with the weaving, she feared she could not see it properly.

"Ah," she said as she spread the great brocade on the grass. "Wang Xing was right; it has almost been like living in my dream house."

Just then, a great wind blew by the weaver's little house, and catching the brocade, it lifted one end up and flung it into the air. Then, blowing steadily, the wind carried the brocade over the hill, and it disappeared into the east.

The weaver gave a scream and tried to follow, but when she got to the crest of the hill and looked to the east, there was no sign of her wonderful brocade.

Clutching her breast, she swooned, falling into the tall grass, where she lay until evening when her sons found her. Carefully, they picked her up and brought her into the house and laid her down upon her pallet.

Zhu held her hand. Shen rubbed her brow with a damp cloth. Wang Xing made some ginger tea, which he got her to drink one small sip at a time. Finally, she slept, and the boys, exhausted from caring for her, slept by her side.

When morning came, the weaver sat up. "Zhu, as you love your mother, go to the east, where the wind went, and find my brocade, for it means more to me than life itself."

Well, Zhu did love her in his own way. So off he went to the east. He put one foot before the other, and within a month he had come to a stone house at the foot of a high mountain.

An old, wrinkled woman with white hair sat on her stone stoop, a stone horse by the door, close to a berry bush.

"Where do you go, young son, and why go in such a hurry?" the old woman asked.

"East," Zhu said.

"Where the sun rises." She nodded at him.

He was so tired he sat down next to her and told her the entire story of the brocade.

"I know that brocade," the old woman told him. She served him a cup of tea.

"Where is it? I must fetch it home," Zhu said.

The old woman held up her hand. "Ah, ah, the fairies of Sun Mountain have carried it away. It is so beautiful, they want to make a copy."

"How can I get it back?" Zhu demanded.

She smiled at him. It did not improve her looks. "The way is difficult."

"I am not a boy to have my knees buckle at the first problem. Tell me. Tell me quickly." His voice shook, though whether with anger or with eagerness, it was difficult to tell.

"Well, first you must knock out those pretty front teeth of yours and put them in the mouth of my stone horse. Then he will be able to eat the red berries hanging in front of him," the old woman said.

At this, Zhu's hand went up to his mouth, but he did not say a word.

She continued. "When the horse has eaten ten berries, you can mount his back and he will carry you over the Mountain of Flame. The fire will sear your feet and burn your hair, but you must not say a word, for to do so will mean your death by that very fire."

Zhu's face went gray. Still he did not say a word.

The old woman went on. "Next you will come to the Ice Sea. The cold will numb your arms and freeze your eyeballs. But if you say a word, you will plunge to the bottom and not come up again."

Zhu's jaw gaped open. And still he did not speak.

The old woman shook her head. "Nah, nah—I can see that you will not be able to stand the test. Never mind. I will give you a small iron box full of gold for coming this far. Take it and live well."

Zhu took the box eagerly and, without a word of thanks, went off, thinking that he had come out of that rather well.

But when he got to the first crossroads, another thought came to his mind: *Why should I share this gold with anyone else? After all, did I not earn it on my own?* And he turned away from the path that led to home and went over the mountain to the city.

The weaver waited for two months for Zhu to return, and the waiting made her ill. She took to her bed and could barely eat.

"Shen, my son," she said at last, "find your brother and the brocade and bring them both back."

So Shen went the same route as Zhu. And he, too, spent a month walking, till he came to the stone house with the stone horse near the berries and the old woman sitting on the stoop.

Like his brother, he turned gray with fear when he learned what he would have to do to get the brocade back. Instead, he took the box of gold the old woman offered, and off he went to the city without a word of thanks. There he found his brother. Together they spent their gold twice as fast as one could have done alone.

Back home, the weaver had spent the months weeping and had made herself blind with grief.

"Mother, let *me* go," said Wang Xing. "I will find the brocade and both my brothers and return with everything to make you happy."

His mother nodded weakly. "But if you, too, do not return, my son, then I will surely die."

Wang Xing did not dawdle like his brothers, and within half a month he arrived at the stone house.

He told the old woman the story of the brocade, and she told him of the fairies. Then she told him all that he would have to do to get the brocade back. At last she said, "But I will gladly give you a box of gold, instead, just as I gave your brothers."

Wang Xing looked closely at the old woman, and if he wondered why she was so eager to send him away, he did not ask. All he said was, "My mother spent three years of her life weaving that brocade. She will die without it. These things you tell me are but small difficulties."

And with that, he knocked out his two front teeth with a stone he found by the old woman's feet. Then he put the teeth into the stone horse's mouth.

Instantly, the horse whinnied and shook its head, walked two steps to the berry bush, and ate ten red berries.

At that, Wang Xing leaped onto the horse's back and away they went, galloping toward the east. Poor Wang Xing had never ridden a horse before, so he held on tight, his hands twisted in the horse's stone-gray mane.

Three days and three nights they galloped, till they came to the foot of the Mountain of Flame. The fire began to sear Wang Xing's feet, and he felt his hair begin to crackle and burn. Setting his lips together so he would not say a word, Wang Xing kicked the horse, and over the mountain they went.

On the other side was the Ice Sea. As the horse waded in, the cold began to numb Wang Xing's legs. As they went deeper in, his arms began to freeze. But once again he set his lips together so he could not say a word, and the horse swam across.

The minute they got to the other side, there was Sun Mountain. Wang Xing knew it because there was a brilliant warm light everywhere and he was no longer cold.

"Up, good horse, to the top of Sun Mountain," he urged.

So up the horse galloped.

At the top of the mountain, it was already night. Yet the moon shone bright enough so that he could see that here was a palace of jade, with jade turrets and jade windows and a great jade door.

Wang Xing knocked on the door, and the door opened by itself. He walked in and saw a hundred fairies sitting at looms, each weaving a small part of a copy of his mother's brocade.

The brocade itself was displayed on a jade pedestal, and it was infinitely more beautiful than anything the fairies were making. Wang Xing felt sorry for the fairies then. For all their magic, they did not have the gift his mother had.

One of the fairies, with hair the color of gold, looked over at Wang Xing. "You have ridden the magic horse over the Mountain of Flame and through the Ice Sea."

"Yes," said Wang Xing.

"Then you are the weaver's son," said another fairy, with hair the color of silver.

"I am."

"We will be done by morning. Will you give us leave to finish?" asked a third fairy, with hair the color of bronze.

He nodded.

They took turns bringing him fairy fruit, as red as the birds in his mother's brocade. He ate and felt refreshed.

"I would like to sleep now," he said. So they made him a bed with the finest silk coverlet and he fell asleep at once. Then they hung a great pearl from the ceiling as a night-light so they could keep on weaving until dawn.

One fairy, with hair the color of midnight, looked at her own work and again at the weaver's brocade. She saw what Wang Xing had seen.

"Ah," she said, "how can I live without the weaver's brocade? If he takes it away, he must take me with it." So she left her own loom and, instead, embroidered a likeness of herself sitting next to a tiny fishpond on the weaver's brocade.

When Wang Xing awoke, the fairies were all gone, vanished like evening stars. But his mother's brocade was still there, under the shining pearl.

He picked up the brocade and clasped it to his chest. Then he leaped onto the horse's back and away they went, across the Ice Sea, over the Mountain of Flame, and to the stone house where the old woman waited.

"You are quite some boy," she said to him. "Both clever and brave."

He looked down at his feet. He did not feel clever or brave—just tired and longing to be home.

When he dismounted, the old woman took the two teeth from the horse and put them back in Wang Xing's mouth.

In an instant, the horse was stone.

"I am sorry for that," said Wang Xing. "He served me well."

"He will serve another some day," the old woman said. "Wait here." She went into her house and came out with a pair of deerskin shoes.

"These will help you get home," she said. "And it will seem to your mother as if you have been gone only a moment. Clap your heels and toes."

Wang Xing put on the shoes, stood, and holding the brocade in his arms, clapped his heels and toes, and in a moment he was home.

Entering the house, he unrolled the brocade in front of his mother's bed.

The brocade gleamed with such a magical light that the old weaver's eyesight was restored at once and she felt full of health.

When she and Wang Xing took the brocade outside to look at it in the light of day, another strange thing happened. The brocade rolled out further and wider until it covered all the land for many lis around. Suddenly all of the threads on the brocade burst into life. The white house stood beside them. The red birds sang in the bushes. Green and gold trees moved in a puzzling breeze. The coiled silver river bubbled and burst its banks. Cows mooed and little lambs frolicked near their ewes. And by a small fishpond sat a lovely maiden with hair as black as midnight, whom neither the weaver nor Wang Xing had ever seen before. It was the fairy who had embroidered herself into the magic brocade.

Wang Xing and the fairy were married, of course, and had seven children, all of whom could weave well. They were taught by their grandmother, who lived with them, honored and adored.

As for the two elder brothers, what of them? Well, one day, two beggars came down the road. They were ragged and tattered, having long ago gambled away all their gold.

They stopped at the white house to beg a bowl of rice from the owner. But when they saw who lived there, happily picnicking in the garden, they were so ashamed they picked up their begging bowls and left, never to return.

ANGOLA

The Young Man Protected by the River

Remember to follow your dream

As the storytellers say: A story, a story. If you would hear it, hush!

Once, in a village that lay on the banks of the Lukala River, there was a man who had five sons and was raising his nephew as well.

Now for many years the uncle was rich, and the five sons had great plans to inherit his wealth. But he fell on hard times, and soon he had little left but a single ox. When he pledged that ox to the headman in the village for some seeds, and those seeds did not sprout and the ox died, the uncle had nothing else to pledge for more seeds but his sons or his nephew.

Naturally, he chose his sister's boy, for his sister—who had died long ago—was not there to call him wicked because of it. As she would. As she surely would.

The boy, whose name was Kingungu, went willing enough. Indeed, what else could he do? He hoped for good treatment from the headman, but, instead, he was beaten badly for small faults and his new master did not clothe him in anything but rags.

Often Kingungu would walk out into the bush and weep, or go down to the river Lukala to gaze out and speak of his dearest wish for a better life—but quietly, for fear his wicked master would hear him and beat him even

11

more. Over the years, he did not complain, nor did he falter in his work, and as he grew older and bigger, he was beaten less often. But he never stopped believing that the day would arrive when his wish would come true.

Now one day he went to sleep, exhausted after the day's work. In his dream, the river spoke to him in a slow voice, saying, "Thou hast come often to my banks and spoken to me of a better life, and I have decided the time for thee to seek it is now. Tomorrow morning, be early at the landing. Three baskets will float by, one great basket, one medium-sized, and one small. Thou shalt take whichever one pleases thee. But as I love thee, I tell thee the best is the *ngonga* basket, the small basket with the tight lid."

Well, Kingungu woke before dawn and thought, *That was but a sleeping dream, and it has little to do with my real life.* So he did not go early to the landing, nor did he go anywhere near the Lukala that day.

That night, he had the same dream. The river spoke to him in its slow way. But when Kingungu awoke, again he thought it but a dream.

The third night was the same.

On the fourth night, the Lukala again spoke, only its voice this time was loud, like a river in spate, like water rushing over stones. "I have told thee and told thee and told thee once again to come down to the landing. Still thou does not come. I do not wait for thee longer. Nor does thy life, Kingungu, which—like a river—rushes on. So, listen and learn."

This time when Kingungu woke, the sky was just beginning to pearl. He got up and walked outside and went down to the landing. Though he still believed all had been just a dream, it was true that his life was rushing away. His boyhood was gone in slavery. If he was to change his life, it had to be now.

Expecting nothing, he stood on the riverbank. Suddenly, down the river floated three baskets.

As they passed him, he saw that the first one was enormous. In it he could see many guns, the muzzles pointing downward and the butt ends up.

If I took that basket, he told himself, *with those guns I could rule this little kingdom. I could kill those who did not obey me. I could seek vengeance on my uncle, who sold me, and on the headman, who is such a hard master.* But this idea did not sit well with him, for although he was a slave, he did not harbor vengeance in his heart, and so he let the large basket float on.

Next came a middle-sized basket, piled so high with cotton cloth that the lid had burst open.

If I took that basket, he told himself, *I could become a merchant. I could sell the cloth for coins and with those coins buy my freedom and a wife and live contentedly all my life. I, too, could own slaves, but I would not treat them badly.* Though that idea did not sit well with him either, for he was not a mercenary young man, and so he let the middle-sized basket float on.

Finally, an *ngonga,* a small basket with a tight lid, floated by. Kingungu remembered the dream river's voice, first sluggish and slow, then like a river in spate, telling him that this basket was the best.

But the ngonga *basket is closed tight,* he told himself. *I do not know what I would be choosing if I pull it out. There may be nothing inside it but air.* He thought again about the guns and then about the cloth. He worried that the Lukala might be a trickster.

But in the end, he trusted his dream and waded into the river. He pulled out the *ngonga* basket and returned home.

The sun was already high overhead, and he knew his master would be angry that he had not yet begun his chores, so he hid the *ngonga* basket in the grass wall of his tiny hut, then went to his master's house.

"Diabu," cried the headman, meaning *you devil,* "why are you late? I will have you beaten."

Kingungu did not want to lie, for he was not a wicked young man, so he said nothing.

"Take up your hoe and go till the soil," said his master. "Then go into the woods and find me some good fire-sticks and bring them back, and mind they are enough. I like a good crackling fire." Then the headman turned away to do his more important business.

Kingungu took the hoe and went to the field, where he spent the rest of the early morning hoeing. He worked extra hard so that the headman

would be pleased. He spent the midday searching the woods for fire-sticks. He found the wood, bound it, and brought it back, carrying the bundle on his head.

When he got to his master's house, the man barely looked up at him. "Go away now, but do not be late again or I will have you beaten."

So Kingungu went back to his own hut. He was so tired from working, he almost fell asleep at once. But, instead, he took the little *ngonga* basket from its hiding place. Slowly, he opened it, not knowing what to expect, and there inside were all manner of things: herbs and cups and thin rope ties, knives and bandages.

"Medicine-things," he called them. He did not even know their names.

"What do I do with all these?" he asked himself. He was not only baffled but a little bit angry as well. "If I had taken the large basket with the guns, I would have known what to do. Or the middle-sized basket with the cloth. But here is a basket full of medicine-things, and I have no skill for healing."

Still, having trusted the river so far, he felt he had to trust it further. That night, when he fell asleep, he opened himself to the dream he knew would come.

In the dream he walked down to the Lukala, and the river spoke in a voice like the tide, going *swee-swash, swee-swash* against the shore.

"Here are the medicine plants you must learn, Kingungu," the river said. "These small ones are for the catarrh in the chest. And these for *ferida*, sores of the body. And these make a poultice for running eyes." On and on the river spoke, and in his dream, Kingungu understood all it taught, and he understood even more that the river would have him be a healer, for that is something that—unlike guns and unlike money—is good for all the people of his world.

In the morning when he rose, Kingungu wondered if he would be able to remember anything the river had said in the dream. He took out the medicine basket again, and suddenly he knew what each plant and each knife was for.

"Aha!" he cried, for now he understood the power of his dream and the life he was to lead.

He went into the field and worked for his master, but he also spent time looking in the grass for more plants from which he could make medicines. He carried his little *ngonga* basket with him everywhere.

Two days later, when Kingungu went back to his master's house to bring him more fire-sticks, carrying the bundle on his head and his *ngonga* basket under one arm, there were two visitors speaking to the headman.

"We have great sickness in our village but no healer, for our last healer was an old man and he has died. We have come a long way looking for someone who can help us."

The master said, "We have no one here for you."

Kingungu waited until the men had left his master's house, then he ran down the road after them. "What sickness is in your village?"

"It is a sickness that brings many sores onto the bodies of our children," they said.

"Will you give me a calling fee if I come and cure your children?" asked Kingungu.

"Are you a healer?" they asked, for they had seen him deliver the fire-sticks to his master, a basket under his arm. His clothes were old and tattered.

"Does this not belong to a healer?" he asked, holding up the little *ngonga* basket. He opened it and showed them the knives and the herbs.

"Perhaps you just found it," said one, for Kingungu did not look to him like someone who would know how to heal.

This was so close to the truth that Kingungu trembled.

By then the master had come over and heard what they had been saying. He said to the men, "This is my slave Kingungu. His uncle gave him to me in payment of a debt many years ago. He is worth little. But if he can cure your children, take him. Promise me, though, that if he fails you will beat him and send him home. That is all he understands. But if he heals your children, you must pay me, for even if he is a healer, he is still my slave."

They nodded, and because they had found no one better, they took Kingungu back to their village.

———

In five days, the children were all well. They ran around the village. They called Kingungu their healer and their friend.

The elders of the village gave Kingungu a heifer in payment, and he went home, where his master took the heifer from him.

"You are my slave," he said, "and what is yours is mine."

Kingungu knew this to be true. He had been sold by his uncle and that could not change unless he could buy himself out of bondage. But he had an idea about that. He said, "Now that I am a healer, I would like to keep half of what I am given."

His master shook his head. "A slave can own nothing."

Kingungu smiled. He knew that the headman was a hard man, but he was a slave to his own greed. It is often thus with the powerful and the rich. They do not just want a lot. They want more. "Then, my master," Kingungu said, "if I cannot keep half of what I earn as a healer, I will do no more healing. I will only hoe and plant and reap for you. I will bring you fire-sticks. There will be no more heifers, only my sweat."

Kingungu knew this would make his master think. At last, the headman nodded. "Then give me half of whatever you make as a healer," he said to Kingungu. "But mind you do not kill anyone with your poor skills."

Kingungu traveled around the country. He was welcome and beloved wherever he went. Where he healed, he always made two heifers his price. One he gave to his master, and one he kept for himself.

In time, Kingungu became rich in cattle, and so he bought himself out of slavery. Then he found a wife and built himself a big house, but he never forgot to treat his servants well. All his dreams were fulfilled, and this because the river had sent him a dream and he had followed it.

As the storytellers say: I have told stories, and if you have heard them—hush! He who has cut wood, binds; he who has done hoeing, leaves work. He who is ready to go, says, "I am going." Finished.

The Devil with the Three Golden Hairs

A generous spirit is better than a strong arm

Once, long ago, there lived a poor woman, the wife of a woodcutter, who longed for a child. When at last she gave birth to a son, he was born with a caul, a membrane, over his head.

The village midwife clapped her hands and called out, "See the caul! That means he shall have great fortune if he lives long enough." And the village wisewoman added loudly, "He shall marry the king's only daughter if he does not die first."

Now it happened that the king was riding through the village in disguise at the very moment of the boy's birth. Riding about in disguise was something he liked to do, to check up on his people, for he was a greedy and crafty man who distrusted them all. He overheard what the midwife and the wisewoman said. It did not please him, for no king wants his only daughter to marry a poor man. But he hid his anger and went in to congratulate the new mother and father.

"If your son is to marry the king's daughter," he said, "it is best he is raised well. Take these gold coins and give me your son. I will see he has the finest education."

The mother would not have it, but her husband said, "If the boy is, indeed, a child of great fortune, perhaps the fortune should start with us." He took the king's money and handed him the child.

The king put the baby in a wooden box and rode off. When he came to a great wide river, he threw the box in. "There," he cried. "Now you will not get the chance to marry my daughter." And away he went without a moment's trouble on his conscience.

But the box did not sink. Instead, it floated along till it came to halt at a milldam. As luck would have it, the miller's apprentice saw it there and, hoping it contained a treasure, pulled the box out with a hook.

What a surprise greeted him! Instead of a treasure, there was a brand-new baby boy sleeping there, his thumb in his mouth like a cork in a bottle.

Since his master had no children of his own and had long wanted a son, the miller's apprentice took the baby to him.

The miller's wife grabbed up the infant and held him tight. "God has given him to us," she said. "What a great fortune!"

Years went by, and the boy grew up handsome and strong. He was honest, generous, hardworking, and kind.

Now one day the king was riding out once again, though this time he was not in disguise. It happened that he stopped at the mill for a drink of cold water and saw the handsome young man who was hard at work fixing the mill wheel.

"Is that your son?" he asked the miller.

The miller told him how the boy had come to them, and if he thought the shock on the king's face was one of delight, he was wrong.

The king knew for certain it was the boy he had thrown away. Being both crafty and wicked, he said at once, "My good miller, may I borrow your son to take a message to the queen?"

"At once, Majesty," replied the miller. A king does not borrow, but commands, of course.

Then the king wrote a hasty note and sealed it. The note said, "As soon as the boy arrives with this letter, you are to have him killed and buried, and all must be done before I return." He gave it to the boy without a moment's trouble on his conscience.

The boy knew nothing of what the sealed letter said, of course. He took it with a quick smile and off he went, though he did not know the way. As he had never been to the city before, he became terribly lost, and night crept on. Afraid to stop for long—because he knew the letter was important—the boy kept going and became even more lost. Still, he put one foot in front of the other until at last he saw a cottage ahead with a light shining faintly in the window.

Perhaps someone within can tell me the way, he thought.

He knocked on the door and a voice called, "Come in."

When he entered, there by the fire sat an old, old lady.

"Good evening, madam," he said. "I was on my way to bring this letter to the queen, but I must confess I am quite lost." He sat down on a bench near her and was suddenly overcome with exhaustion.

"Lost entirely," the old woman told him, "for this is a den of thieves. When they come home, if they find you, they will kill you."

"Then perhaps, dear madam," the boy said, "with your permission, I will rest for just a moment, for I am too tired to go a step more." He stretched out on the bench, meaning just to close his eyes, and fell instantly to sleep.

Not an hour later, the robbers came home and saw the boy lying there.

"Do not kill him," said the old lady, who was the mother of that wicked crew. "He called me madam and he has such a pretty face." Then she told them about the letter for the queen.

They opened the letter at once, and saw what the king had written. Immediately they felt pity for the boy, for wasn't he as much an outlaw as they?

"Tear up the letter," said the chief of the robbers, "and I will write a new one." And he wrote, "As soon as the boy arrives with this letter, you are to marry him to our daughter, and all must be done before I return."

The robbers laughed at this, for they thought it a great prank to play on the king, who had outlawed them all. Then they ate quickly and were gone again.

When the boy awoke, he was grateful to be alive. "What good fortune I have," he said. Then he kissed the old lady's hand, called her dear madam one more time, grabbed up his letter, and was away.

Now when the boy arrived at the palace, the queen read the letter not once but twice. It surprised her, for it was unlike her husband, who was not a nice man.

Then she did as the letter directed, preparing a splendid wedding feast.

The princess liked the looks of the young man and was delighted that her father had arranged for him to be her husband. So they immediately began their honeymoon in joy and happiness.

The king was some time returning home, and when he arrived and found that the boy was married to his only daughter, he was furious. "How can this be?" he roared.

When the queen showed him the letter, he turned red in the face.

"Stupid woman!" he called the queen.

"Faithless daughter!" he called the princess.

Then he summoned the young man to him.

Now the boy knew better than to call the king "Father," and he bowed very low as his wife had taught him.

"Now, my boy," said the king in a false voice, "do you not know that he who would marry my daughter must go north and fetch me three golden hairs from the Devil's head?"

"I had not heard that, Majesty," said the boy. "But I will go at once."

"But, my dear," said his new young bride, "are you not afraid?" She herself was very much afraid. She knew her father to be a villain.

"I am not afraid," he told her, "for it is clear to me that I am a child of great fortune. Who but someone of great fortune could be married to such a wonderful wife?" He took a fond farewell of her, then off he went, though he did not know the way.

The boy walked and walked north for miles, and came at last to a city

21

where a tall watchman at the gate asked him who he was and what his trade.

"I have no trade," the boy admitted, for a prince has none. "But I have good fortune in all I do."

"Then, child of fortune," said the watchman, "perhaps you can help us with ours, for it is all bad. Our market fountain, which once flowed with both water and wine, has dried up. Now not even water comes out."

"I will have an answer for you when I have been to get the three golden hairs from the Devil," the boy said.

Off he went again to the north and came to another town, where a short gatekeeper asked him who he was and what his trade.

"I have no trade," the boy admitted. "But I have good fortune in all I do."

"Then, child of fortune," said the gatekeeper, "perhaps you can help us with ours, for it is all bad. Tell us why the tree in our town square, which once bore golden apples, now doesn't even have leaves."

"I will have an answer for you when I have been to get the three golden hairs from the Devil," the boy told him.

He walked even further north and came to a great river. A ferryman with long gray hair and an even longer gray beard asked him who he was and what his trade.

"I have no trade," the boy admitted. "But I have good fortune in all I do."

"Then, child of fortune," said the ferryman, "perhaps you can help me with mine, for it is all bad. I must row back and forth, forth and back across the river and cannot seem to get free of my boat."

"I will have an answer for you when I have been to get the three golden hairs from the Devil," the boy said.

"Then I will know soon enough," said the ferryman, "for on the other side of this river is the entrance to Hell. Climb aboard and I will row you over."

So the boy climbed in, and in a twinkling, the ferryman had rowed him across.

The entrance to Hell was black and sooty, and the inside worse. The boy walked right into the Devil's own chamber, but the Devil himself was not home. Only his grandmother was there, an impish-looking old woman knitting a long, dark strand.

"What do you want?" she asked.

"Oh, dear madam, my father-in-law, the king, says I must get three golden hairs from the Devil's head," said the boy, "else I cannot remain married to his daughter."

"Hmmm," said the old woman, and put down her knitting. "You are asking for a lot, and if the Devil comes home and finds you here, he will eat you. But as you have called me madam, I will take pity on you." She waved the strand of knitting at him and turned him into an ant.

If you are wondering how that helped him, you must listen further.

"Here, ant," said the Devil's grandmother, "creep into the folds of my dress, and I will keep you safe."

"Thank you, dear madam," said the boy. "And by the way, could you also get the Devil to answer three questions?"

"Hmmm," said the old woman. "Lucky you called me madam again. All right, I can but try."

So he told her the three questions—about the fountain that used to flow water and wine, the tree that used to bear golden apples, and the ferryman who had to row back and forth ceaselessly.

"Those are difficult questions, indeed," said the Devil's grandmother. "But if anyone knows the answers, it is Himself. So it will be your job to be quiet and listen and pay attention when I pull out those hairs."

Not an hour later, the Devil came home, grousing and grumping over what a hard day he had had. No sooner had he put a cloven hoof into the house than he stopped and sniffed.

"I smell man."

"You *always* smell man," his grandmother said. "It comes from all your toil with wicked souls. The odor gets up your nose. Sit down and eat your dinner."

So the Devil ate and drank, and ate some more. Then, tired, he lay down with his head on his grandmother's lap so she could comb his hair free of sweat tangles.

Soon he was fast asleep and snoring.

Then the old woman took hold of one golden hair, and *snip-snap,* she pulled it out and set it on the bench beside her.

"Ouch!" said the Devil, sitting up. "What are you doing?"

"I had a bad dream," said his grandmother. "I dreamed I was in a town that had a fountain that used to flow both water and wine and now no longer flows at all."

"Ho!" said the Devil. "You have dreamed a true dream. There is such a place. If the townsfolk but knew it, they would find a toad under a stone in the well. If they kill the toad, both water and wine will flow again." Then he lay back down and was soon snoring again.

Then the old woman took hold of another golden hair, and *snip-snap,* she pulled it out and set it on the bench beside her.

"Ouch!" said the Devil, sitting up again. "What are you doing?"

"I had another bad dream," said his grandmother. "This time I dreamed I was in a town where there stood a tree that once bore golden apples but now no longer even bears leaves."

"Ho!" said the Devil. "You have dreamed another true dream. There is such a place. If the townsfolk but knew it, they would find a mouse in a burrow under the tree. He is gnawing on the roots. All they need to do is kill the mouse and the tree will flower again. But take care that you do not wake me another time, or I shall have to box your ears." He lay back down and once again began to snore.

His grandmother waited until he was fast asleep. Then she took hold of a third golden hair, and *snip-snap,* she pulled it out and set it on the bench beside her.

"Ouch!" said the Devil, sitting up again. "Didn't I warn you? I shall have to box your ears."

"Now, grandson, it was only another bad dream," she said, and kissed him on the forehead.

The Devil smiled. He loved his grandmother and had only been kidding about boxing her ears.

"I had a third bad dream," said his grandmother. "This time I dreamed I was at the river across from the entrance to our home. The ferryman was going ceaselessly back and forth. And, oh, he was tired and wanted to stop."

"Ho!" said the Devil. "You have dreamed yet another true dream. But the ferryman is such a fool. All he has to do is wait until the next person comes to the shore, wanting to go across. Then he must put the oar in his passenger's hand and leap from the boat. Then he will be free and his passenger will have to take his place. Now let me sleep, old woman. No more dreams."

"No more dreams," she agreed. "I think three is the charm."

And the Devil fell to snoring.

As soon as he was fast asleep, the old woman took the ant from the folds of her dress and turned him back into a human again.

"You have your three golden hairs and your three answers," she said. "Now be quick, child of fortune, and be off."

The boy thanked the Devil's grandmother profusely, and with the three golden hairs clutched in his hand, away he went.

When he came to the ferryman, he said, "I have your answer. But first row me over and you shall have it." When they were safely on the other side and the boy on the shore, he told the ferryman what to do.

Then he walked south till he came to the town in which the short gatekeeper stood guard. "Kill the mouse that gnaws the roots of the tree," he said. And when that was done, and the tree bloomed with golden apples, the town gave him two donkeys laden with gold.

Then he walked south again till he came to the town in which the tall watchman stood guard. "Kill the toad that lives in the well." When that was done, both water and wine flowed swiftly from the fountain once again, and the town gave him two more donkeys laden with gold.

At last, he walked south until he came back to the king's palace.

His wife, the princess, kissed him. The queen gave him a great big hug.

However, the king was astonished to see him alive, with the three golden hairs from the Devil's head. He was even more astonished to see the four donkeys laden with gold.

"Where did you get such wealth?" the king asked.

The child of fortune looked at the king. He knew the king's greedy heart, and in that moment he understood what a villain stood before him. For a long moment he did not answer. Then he said carefully, "Far to the north there is a great river. I was rowed across by a ferryman. On the other side is a dark shore covered with gold instead of sand."

"Can I fetch some, too?" asked the king.

"As much as you like," said the boy. He hoped he guessed correctly how things would end.

Without waiting for his guards—perhaps he feared they might make off with the treasure themselves—the greedy king set off on his own. He went north as fast as his horse could carry him. When he came to the river, he called for the ferryman to row him across. The ferryman came to the near shore, helped the king in, set the oar in the king's hand, and leaped from the boat. He got on the king's horse and off he rode. From that day on, the king had to ferry back and forth, forth and back—a just punishment for his wrongdoings.

As for the boy, he took the four donkeys loaded with gold to the miller and his wife so that they—his adopted parents—might share in his new-found wealth, for he was as generous as he was lucky.

Then he ruled the kingdom with his lovely queen by his side, and brought all of his people—highborn and low—good fortune indeed.

NORWAY

Eating with Trolls

Do not confuse a quiet thinker with a ne'er-do-well

Once upon a time, on a poor farm by the side of a forest, lived an old farmer and his three sons.

Now the farmer was feeble with age, and his sons were little help. The oldest two were boasters, and the third was called Ash Lad because he spent his time sitting by the hearth covered with ashes.

Well, things went from bad to worse: not enough rain or too much rain, not enough frost or too much frost. Wind and sun came at the wrong times. Spring was rough and summer rougher. Soon the farm was ruined.

The only thing worth a penny was the wood in the nearby forest, so the farmer called his sons to him.

"We must chop down some of those trees," he told them, "and sell the wood. It is the only way for us to live."

Well, that seemed too much like work to the boys.

The old man reasoned with them. And then he argued with them. Finally, when there was nothing else to do, he threatened to send them into the world, where they would have to make a living on their own.

At last they saw the wisdom of his words.

"I will go, Father," said the eldest, a lad named Ole. His mother made him

28

a basket filled with hard cheese and soft bread, and off he went to the edge of the woods.

No sooner had he started chopping on a small, shaggy fir tree—one not much bigger than a pile of kindling, really—than a burly troll stomped out of the forest.

The troll was nine feet tall and nine feet wide. He had a nose like a ski jump and skin as gray as dried wood. When he got close to the boy, the troll rolled his saucer eyes and thundered:

> *"He who dares chop down Troll's trees*
> *Will be cut off below the knees.*
> *Stop at once, or I will stop you myself."*

He held up a fist as large as a log.

Well, Ole did not have to be told twice. He flung away his ax and ran for home. When he got there safely, he told his mother and father what had happened.

His mother patted his hand and smoothed his brow.

But his father said, "Pah! What a ninny. The trolls never stopped me from chopping when I was young. Besides, it's said that trolls keep stolen gold in their houses. Gold that belongs to all the people in this kingdom. You should have beaten him up and brought the treasure home."

The next day it was the second son's turn.

This boy was Rolle. His mother made him a basket filled with hard cheese and soft bread, and off he went to the edge of the woods.

Trembling, he began to cut that same shaggy fir. But no sooner had the ax bit into the wood than the troll stomped out, rolling his saucer eyes and thundering:

> *"He who dares chop down Troll's trees*
> *Will be cut off below the knees.*
> *Stop at once, or I will stop you myself."*

He held up a fist as big as a mattress.

Well, Rolle threw away his ax and left the basket behind, and he ran home faster than the first. When he got home and told the tale, his mother patted his hand and smoothed his brow.

But his father said, "Pah! What a ninny. Not only a ninny, but a nitwit. The trolls never stopped me from chopping when I was young. Besides, it's said that trolls keep stolen gold in their houses. Gold belonging to all the people in this kingdom. You should have beaten him up and brought the treasure home."

On the third day, it was Ash Lad's turn.

"You?" Ole laughed. "You have never been beyond the door."

"Or washed the ashes out of your hair," said Rolle.

"Well, I will go will ye, nil ye," said Ash Lad. "Just give me a lunch, Mother, and I will be away."

His mother hadn't expected him to go, and she was out of hard cheeses and soft bread. In fact, there was only a freshly curdled cheese to give him, still runny with whey, and no bread at all. There was no basket left, either, for both had been left by Ash Lad's brothers in the forest.

"I will take my grandad's old knapsack," said Ash Lad. So he packed the runny cheese in his knapsack and away he went.

Halfway to the forest, Ash Lad came upon a little bird that had knocked itself silly flying into a tree. He put it into his shirt, close by his heart, so it could stay warm till it was ready to fly again.

Then off he strode to the forest's edge, where he found that same shaggy fir, with two big chips out of its side.

Ash Lad set down his knapsack and took up his ax.

No sooner had his blade bit into the wood than out came the troll once again, his great saucer eyes rolling. He thundered:

> "He who dares chop down Troll's trees
> Will be cut off below the knees.
> Stop at once, or I will stop you myself."

30

He held up a fist as big as a front door.

Now Ash Lad may never have gone away from the hearth before, but it was not because he was dumb. He had given the problem of trolls a great deal of thought. There is, after all, not much to do besides think when you are squatting by the fire day and night, night and day.

He knew that trolls were strong and trolls were mean. But he also knew that trolls were stupid.

"Do not kill me over a tree," he said to the troll. "Let's have a wager, instead."

The troll stopped in his tracks. "A wager?" Trolls loved to bet. "What can I win?"

"If you win, you eat me. And if I win, I eat you," said Ash Lad.

"But I can eat you anyway," said the troll.

"Do not pick your teeth before a meal," said Ash Lad. He set down the ax.

"What is the game?" asked the troll.

"High, strong, and fill your belly," said Ash Lad.

The troll liked the sound of that. "How is it played?"

"One, two, and three," said Ash Lad. "One—whoever throws a stone farthest wins the first part. Two—whoever squeezes a stone hardest wins the second part. Three—whoever eats the most wins all."

The troll grinned. He knew trolls were stronger than humans. And bigger eaters, too. "Done!" he said, and spit in his hand to seal the wager.

They shook hands, troll and lad, and the boy's hand was nearly lost in the troll's vast palm.

"Pick out a stone and fling it as high as you can," said Ash Lad. "As I know I am better, you go first."

The troll looked around and found a rock on the ground. It was bigger than Ash Lad's head. Picking the stone up, the troll reared back, and flung it into the sky. It cleared the tops of the tallest trees, hesitated for a moment near a mountaintop, then fell back to earth with a sound like a cannon shot.

"Beat that," said the troll, licking his lips. He could already taste Ash Lad.

Ash Lad bent over, making a pretense of looking around. Then he put his hand inside his shirt, pulling out the little bird, which was nicely recovered from its knockabout.

Rearing back, just as the troll had done, Ash Lad flung the bird into the sky. Before the troll could make it out, the bird was but a speck against the blue. It went past the tallest trees, past the mountaintops, and into the protection of the clouds.

"Well," said Ash Lad, hand shading his eyes as he stared into the sky and pretending he could still see the stone bird, "that stone might not come down for days. I guess I win the first part."

"You were lucky," said the troll. He was not happy and he ground his teeth. It was a sound like distant thunder. "But I will beat you this time. Trolls are stronger than anyone else. I will pick up a stone and squeeze it till the water runs out."

He found a gray boulder and picked it up, then squeezed, and squeezed, and squeezed some more. The stone began to crumble.

"Not bad," said Ash Lad. He bent over, making a pretense of looking around for a stone of his own. Then he put his hand in his knapsack and got out the cheese, which was an off-white color and as round as a stone. He squeezed it between his hands until the whey spurted out.

"I guess I win the second part," said Ash Lad, putting his knapsack on his back. "Time for our last contest."

The troll looked troubled. "Where shall we eat?"

"Why, at your house," said Ash Lad, thinking about the treasure stored there.

The troll knew that no one can outeat a troll, especially in his own house, so he was pleased with Ash Lad's answer. He put the boy into his shirt pocket and off they went, deep into the forest, where the troll cave had been dug into the mountainside.

The troll's house was enormous and the hearth even bigger.

"I will make up the fire," said the troll, "if you fetch the water for the porridge pot." He pointed to two iron buckets that were the size of barrels.

"Those thimbles?" Ash Lad said. "Not worth dragging them along. I will go and fetch the entire well."

Oh, dear, thought the troll. *I do not dare lose my well.* So he said to Ash Lad, "Never mind. You make up the fire and I will fetch the water."

"As you wish," said Ash Lad, though it was just what he had hoped.

As soon as the troll went outside, Ash Lad took his knapsack and tied it around his front, covering it up with his shirt. Then he made up the fire and had it roaring away by the time the troll returned with the iron buckets brimful of water.

The troll set the buckets onto the fire, and when the water began to boil, he scattered handfuls of porridge flakes in and stirred with a wooden spoon that was as tall as Ash Lad and as big around.

"So let us have that eating match now," said Ash Lad.

The troll's saucer eyes got huge. "If you win," he told Ash Lad, "I shall leave you alone. And if I win, I shall eat you."

"Fair enough," said Ash Lad. "I am mighty hungry!"

Then the two of them tucked into the porridge, though most of what Ash Lad took he scooped down the neck of his shirt and into the sack beneath.

When the knapsack was quite full, Ash Lad took out his knife and ripped a gash through his shirt and through the knapsack, and the porridge spilled out onto the floor.

"Ah, that's better," Ash Lad said. "Give me more." He took spoonful after spoonful. "And more."

The poor troll tried to keep up with him, but it was no good. "I cannot manage another bite." He put his hand on his stomach and groaned.

"Do as I do," Ash Lad advised, holding up his knife.

"But doesn't it hurt dreadfully?" asked the troll.

"Hardly at all," said Ash Lad.

So the troll did as the boy said, only, of course, he had no knapsack to slice, only his poor belly.

And—*spit-spat!*—that was the end of him.

As for Ash Lad, he found gold and silver in the troll's house, all that had been stolen from the villages for miles around. He brought the treasure home, shared it with everyone in the little kingdom, and still had plenty left over to

pay off his family's debt. Everyone called him a hero. They drank great toasts of ale to him and patted him on the back. They would have made him king.

But Ash Lad wanted none of that. He just went back to his fire, where he sat day and night, night and day, thinking. After all, it was his hard thinking and clever mind that had defeated the troll. He wanted to be ready for the next time.

AFRICAN AMERICAN

Knee-High Man

Height does not make a hero

In a swamp not far from here lived Knee-High Man, and he was as little as his name sounds. He was knee-high to a reed and knee-high to a hoptoad. He was a small man, but he wanted to be sizable.

So one day, he decided to go calling on the biggest critter in the neighborhood to find out how to make himself big.

Off he went to visit Mr. Horse.

"Hey, brother," he cried out in his knee-high voice, somewhere between a squeak and a squawk. "How can I grow as big as you?"

Horse turned his great head till he eyed Knee-High Man. "Eat a whole mess o' corn," he said. "Then run all day." He whinnied and went back to his eating.

Well, Knee-High Man did just what the horse advised, but it was no dang good. The corn hurt his little belly, and the running hurt his little legs. Instead of getting bigger, why, the Knee-High Man was sure he'd gotten smaller.

"That brother didn't do me any favors," said the Knee-High Man. "I'd better get advice from somebody else."

So off he went to visit Mr. Bull.

"Hey, brother," he cried out in his knee-high voice, somewhere between a whisper and a whimper. "How can I grow as big as you?"

Bull looked down till they were eye to eye. "Eat grass," he said, "and learn to bellow."

Well, Knee-High Man did just what the bull advised, but it still was no dang good. The grass hurt his little belly, and the bellowing made his little throat sore. Instead of getting bigger, why, the Knee-High Man was sure he'd gotten even smaller.

"That brother didn't do me any favors," said Knee-High Man. "I'd better get advice from somebody else."

So off he went to visit Mr. Owl. Owl was known for his wisdom, even though he wasn't near that big himself. He was a preacher, too, which made him somebody important.

"Hey, brother," Knee-High Man cried out in his knee-high voice, somewhere between a hough and a howl.

"Whooooo are you?" asked owl.

"I am Knee-High Man," Knee-High Man explained. "But I am tired of being small. How can I grow big? I want to be sizable, like Mr. Horse or like Mr. Bull—only not made to eat corn and run all day, or to eat grass and bellow."

Owl looked at Knee-High Man with his great eyes. "Why do you want to be big, brother? Is it because folks are picking fights with you all the time?"

Knee-High Man shook his head. "No."

"Is it because you want to see a long way?" asked Owl.

"No."

"Because you want to carry heavy objects?" asked Owl.

"No."

"Well," Owl said, "there's no reason to be bigger in the body than anyone else, Knee-High Man. But there's reason enough to be bigger in the *brain*!" He flapped his wings—soft and silent—and flew off.

Knee-High Man thought about that, and the more he thought, the bigger in the brain he became, till at last he was well satisfied. Then he went back to his swamp, never to mind his height again.

RUSSIA

Language of the Birds

Not all enchantments are wicked

In a certain city in a certain country whose name begins with an *R*—lived a merchant, his wife, and their little son, Vasili, who was six years old.

One day the three of them were sitting down to supper. The table was laid with all manner of sweetmeats and sweet breads, and the samovar was bubbling away on the tiled stove. In a cage by the window, a nightingale sang a song as bubbly as the samovar, but sad, too, as if it mourned being in the cage.

"Ah," said the merchant. "If only I could know what the bird is saying. I would give the one who could translate for me half of my possessions while I live, and the whole of it at the moment of my death." He spoke extravagantly because he did not expect an answer.

Little Vasili spoke up. "Papa," he said, "I know what the nightingale says, only I fear to speak it aloud."

"Speak and do not be afraid," said his father. "Have you ever been punished for speaking aloud?"

"Indeed, speak," said his mother. "Papa and I will not be angry, whatever it is you say." They doted on the boy, who was gentle and wise beyond his years.

So, eyes shining with tears, Vasili said, "Dear Papa, dear Mama, the nightingale speaks of a time when you two will be my servants. It says that one day soon Papa will draw me water and Mama will give me a towel to wipe my face and hands. And you shall both bow in my direction and call me *Sir*."

The merchant looked at his wife and she at him. This did not sound like their sweet Vasili.

"Who is this child, that we should soon be his servants? What nonsense." The merchant glowered at his son.

"But it is true, Papa." Vasili's tears ran like rivers down his cheeks.

"Go to bed," the merchant said. "We will speak of this no more." Though his voice was calm, the merchant was furious. A hard line ran between his eyebrows, and his eyes were like cold silver balls.

While Vasili slept in his little wooden bed, the merchant said to his wife, "Though I have never seen it before, there is something wrong with the boy. He has been enchanted by an evil fairy. We must send him far away from here or the enchantment will fall upon us as well."

The merchant's wife began to weep. "No, no, my husband, we cannot do such a thing."

"But remember what he said," the merchant reminded her, "and the cold way he said it. Surely he has been cursed by a wicked fairy."

The merchant's wife nodded. She, too, had been afraid of the way Vasili had spoken. "Imagine!" she cried. "A father and mother to wait upon their child like servants."

"Unnatural!" the merchant said.

So it was agreed. They got a little boat and, in the middle of the night, put the sleeping boy in it and sent it out onto the great wide sea. For good measure, they opened the door to the nightingale's cage. Then they shook it until the bird fled, flying off toward the water, where at last it found the little boat and alighted on the sleeping boy's shoulder.

The boat sailed on and on till morning, when it approached a far shore. There, men on a great ship—its sails spread wide—found the little boat bobbing like a cork on the waves.

"Look, captain, look!" the sailors cried. They drew the little boat up, and there was the sleeping boy.

The captain, who had no children of his own, sat with the child till he awoke. When Vasili opened his eyes, he was bright and cheerful. Immediately he got up and offered to help aboard ship. Not once did he let a sad or mournful word drop from his lips. The captain was so taken by the boy, he decided to adopt Vasili and raise him up as his own son.

The very next evening, the nightingale sang in its tremulous voice, and Vasili turned to his new father.

"Papa," he said, "I understand the language of birds. The nightingale says there is a storm brewing that will break the masts of your ship and scatter all your sails. We must go back to shore."

"Nay, little one," the captain said. "No one can understand the language of birds. You are making that up."

Well, sure enough, there was a great storm. The winds blew so furiously, the masts of the boat were shattered and the sails scattered.

"These things happen," said the captain to Vasili. "The sea is a hard master and a soft mistress."

The sailors rebuilt the masts and resewed the sails, and off they went again, on the great wide sea.

A week later, Vasili once again listened to the nightingale singing. "Papa," he said, "the nightingale says there are twelve pirate ships coming toward us, and they will take us prisoner if we do not change our course."

"Twelve pirate ships?" the captain asked.

"And two have large black flags," the boy insisted.

Well, this time the captain believed the boy and returned to shore. He watched through his spyglass as twelve ships went by. The flagship bore a black flag and the last ship bore another.

The captain turned to the boy and said, "Never fear telling me what your little nightingale sings, child. I will always listen."

———

When the pirate ships were long gone, the captain and his crew, along with little Vasili, sailed off again. They came at last to the city of *K—*, where the king and his wife and child had had no rest, neither by day nor by night. The trouble was that three crows harassed them at the window of whatever room they were in.

Everything had been tried to drive off the crows. Guns had been shot off. Traps had been set. Nets, lines, dogs. There had been hawkers and huntsmen, poachers and poisoners. Nothing had worked, and the king had become exceedingly cranky and tired.

So he had signs set at every crossroads and harbor stating:

If any man can drive away the crow and its wife and child, the king will grant that man half the kingdom and his youngest daughter as wife. However, if a man tries and does not succeed, he will forfeit his head.

When the captain and his crew landed and read the sign, they were excited. But when they saw all the heads of the hawkers and huntsmen, poachers and poisoners who had tried and failed, they decided to leave.

All except Vasili. "Papa," he cried out, "let me go and help the king."

"No," the captain said. "Never."

But Vasili pleaded. "Because I can understand the language of birds, perhaps I will succeed where others have failed."

No became *maybe.*

So Vasili entreated. "I knew about the storm and about the pirate ships, and other things besides. Surely I can help this poor family, for no kingdom should be ruled by a king who is exceedingly cranky and tired."

"Very well then," said the captain. "But if you come to harm, the blame is on your own head. And that head off on a stake. I will not stay to see it." He gathered his men and sailed away.

So Vasili went along to the palace by himself, and because he was so young, he was allowed right in.

Once there, he told the king, "I can help you, Your Majesty, because I understand the language of birds. Now you must open all the windows."

The king smiled and, as if to humor the boy, did what was asked. "Open all the windows," he ordered. Servants throughout the palace jumped to do his bidding.

Then Vasili went to the windows and leaned out. The three crows were screaming at one another—an argument that went on and on. When he had heard what the crows had to say, Vasili turned to the king.

"And what are the crows telling you, young master?" asked the king, smiling.

"They are arguing over which the youngest crow belongs to, sire, the father or the mother," said Vasili. "And they are appealing—as they have been all along, if only you could have understood them—to you, whose wisdom is so great."

"Is that all?" asked the king. "Then tell them the little crow belongs to the father. Maybe that will satisfy them."

Vasili went back to the window and told the crows, and the little crow flew to the left with his father, the mother crow flew to the right, and they were gone.

The king was so relieved to be shed of the noisy crows that he took Vasili to live with him in the palace. He wanted to raise Vasili as a son, for the boy was too young yet to marry anyone, even the youngest princess, who was but six herself.

Vasili was delighted, and before long he and the princess were the best of friends. And after that, they loved each other truly.

And after *that*—

In ten years, when they were old enough—the two were wed, and Vasili received half the kingdom as his wedding present.

One day, however, Vasili decided it would be wonderful to sail around the world. The king outfitted a ship with sails of silver and gold, and off Vasili went.

In one city, he stayed the night in the home of a rich merchant, getting there too late to have supper with his hosts and being waited on only by the servants.

In the morning when he rose, he told the valet, "I wish to wash."

The merchant, wishing to curry favor with the wealthy prince who sailed in so fine a ship, came in with the water himself. His wife brought in the towels.

When Vasili saw them, his heart remembered what his head had forgotten. They were his true mama and papa. He threw his arms around the startled couple.

"Do you remember little Vasili?" he cried. "Do you remember the nightingale?"

They nodded.

"I am that boy. And what the bird prophesied has all come true."

They hugged and kissed him and would not let him go, for they had long since repented of their wickedness and had always hoped that one day they would see their beloved son again.

Vasili forgave them and brought them back with him in the ship that had sails of silver and gold. They lived at the palace with Vasili and his princess wife.

Years later, when Vasili was made king, his mama and papa always listened to his pronouncements with care.

"If he is under an enchantment," his mama always said, "it is by a good fairy."

"Very good," said his papa. And they played with their grandchildren for the rest of their long lives.

Thick-Head

The one who laughs last is the hero

Once, long ago, three brothers lived with their widowed mother in a village near the sea. They had no other relatives. Because of this, they did not dwell in the longhouse with others of their tribe, but in a wigwam far apart. Further, they had little to eat but what they could get for themselves, and often they had to go deep into the forest for game. Because of this, the oldest two brothers soon became the best hunters in the village.

However, the youngest boy was small and weak, and so he was never allowed to go along on these hunting trips. Instead, he had to stay home gathering wood and carrying water—women's work.

The older brothers called the younger brother Thick-Head. Soon everyone in the longhouse called him that as well.

"Do not worry, my son," his mother told him. "They laugh at you now, but you'll prove wiser than any of them."

"Do you mean it, Mother?" Thick-Head asked.

"We will see. We will see," was all she answered.

Now the sagamore, the chief of the village, had a beautiful daughter. Many men wished to marry her, including Thick-Head's older brothers. But the sagamore said, "My daughter is too young now. When she is old enough, I will not pick the richest or the strongest among you for her husband. I will pick the young man who can make the greatest profit from hunting."

The brothers talked among themselves.

"Am I not a great hunter of deer?" said the oldest brother.

"Am I not a greater hunter of beaver and otter?" said the middle brother.

"I am better," said the first.

"No, I am better," said the other.

They quarreled for a day and a night, until they decided to go into the woods and prove which one was right.

"Let me go, too," begged Thick-Head. "I have never been in the deep forest."

"No!" the older brothers cried. "You will bring us bad luck."

But their mother insisted, so they had to take Thick-Head with them.

However, Thick-Head was not a burden. In fact, they left him alone in the woods. The hunting that day was good. The brothers came back so laden with deer and rabbit, otter and beaver, that water almost swept over the sides of the canoe.

All that Thick-Head brought home was a large earthworm. It was a strange pink color, like a sunrise, and as thick around as his finger, as long as his arm.

"See, Mother, what a fool he is," the brothers said.

"He will surprise you yet," she told them.

The older brothers shook their heads. Then, leaving but a small bit of the game for their mother and Thick-Head, they took the rest to show the sagamore. They wanted him to see that they were hunters who could make a great profit.

While his brothers were away, Thick-Head put his earthworm in a pen, and a large duck came waddling by. Sticking her bill over the top of the pen, she gobbled up the worm.

This made Thick-Head very sad, but it made him angry, too. He followed the duck back to its owner, who lived in the longhouse.

"Your duck ate my worm!" Thick-Head cried. "That worm was the only thing I brought back from a long day's hunting."

The duck's owner shook his head. He did not want the boy to be unhappy. "Let me give you something in exchange."

"I only want my worm," said Thick-Head.

"The duck has eaten it. It is gone forever."

"It is not gone forever," said Thick-Head. "It is in the duck's belly. Give me the duck."

They argued back and forth for some time, until at last the man said, "What is the use of arguing with a fool?" And he gave the duck to Thick-Head.

Thick-Head put the duck in the pen where the worm had been and tied a large rock to its foot so it could not fly away. "Now I have both my worm *and* a duck," he said. "And that is a good profit!"

That very afternoon, a fox came along and saw the duck. In a minute, the fox was over the pen. The duck quacked and squawked and beat its wings trying to get away, but the fox soon silenced it. The fox was just licking the last bits of feather from its lips when Thick-Head came running from the wigwam.

"That is my duck," he cried, "which I got when it ate my worm, which was the only thing I had gotten from a long day's hunting." Grabbing the fox, he tied it up and threw it into the pen.

"This is not bad at all," Thick-Head told himself. "Now I have my worm, and the duck, and a fox as well. Not a bad profit!"

That night, an old and hungry wolf came through the forest. In the moon's silver light, the wolf saw the fox in the pen, tied up and unable to run away. In a moment, the wolf leaped into the pen and ate up every last bit of the fox, even the red tail.

Thick-Head heard the wolf crunching the fox bones. He ran outside. With one blow of an ax he split the wolf in two.

"Now," he told his brothers, "here is profit indeed. I have the worm, the duck, the fox—and the wolf as well."

"What a Thick-Head," said the eldest. "You have nothing at all but a dead wolf."

"Before two days are passed, that will be a dead, *smelly* wolf," added the other.

"You must bury that wolf," they said together.

Instead of burying the wolf, Thick-Head skinned it, dried the skin, and made a drum. He beat the drum all the next morning, singing:

> *"My drum is a wolf drum.*
> *My drum is a fox drum.*
> *My drum is a duck drum.*
> *My drum is a worm."*

The sagamore heard Thick-Head playing on the drum and said to him, "Let me borrow your drum. I wish to announce that my daughter is finally old enough to be married. That is the best-sounding drum in the village."

Thick-Head could not very well refuse the sagamore, but he said, "Be careful. Do not tear my drum. My worm and my duck and my fox and my wolf all helped make it. It is my only treasure. There is not another one like it."

"I will treat it well," said the sagamore.

The next morning, Thick-Head went to the longhouse to get his drum, but when he got there, he saw that the drumhead was split. It could never be played again.

"I know you treasured the drum," said the sagamore. "So I will give you many beaver pelts and many otter pelts in payment. I will give you dried venison and salmon."

"I do not want those things," said Thick-Head. "I want my drum back. My worm and my duck and my fox and my wolf are all in it."

The sagamore shook his head. "I cannot give the drum back to you. But I will give you whatever you name."

Thick-Head smiled. He thought, *I had a duck for a worm, a fox for a duck, a wolf for a fox, a drum for a wolf. There is nothing I cannot do.* Then he said aloud, "Then I name your daughter in marriage."

"My daughter!" the sagamore cried. But he had given his word. Everyone in the longhouse had heard him do it.

"After all, I deserve to be your daughter's husband," said Thick-Head. "I have turned a worm into a marriage—have I not made the greatest profit in hunting?"

So Thick-Head moved into the longhouse with the sagamore's family, along with his mother and brothers, and he and the sagamore's daughter were soon married.

And if he never went hunting again, she did not complain, for he was already known throughout the tribe as a great hunter.

As for Thick-Head's brothers, they never quite forgave him for marrying the sagamore's daughter. But whenever they complained, their mother reminded them, "Did I not say he would surprise you all?"

BURMA

The Fisherman and the Chamberlain

Brave beats greedy every time

Long ago, there was a king who would eat only fried fish. Kings alone are allowed such delicacies.

Now one day, there were such terrible storms that none of the fishermen could catch anything, and so all that day, the king had to go hungry.

A hungry king is not a happy king. He gave an order to his chamberlain: "Announce by gong and drum that anyone who brings me even a single fingerling will be given whatever reward he names."

The chamberlain went out and announced this near and far, but still no boats would go out into the storm.

As evening set in, one young fisherman stood by the shore of the roiling sea. He did not go out in his boat but cast a line into the waves.

What should he catch but a nice big fish with silver fins and a long fat tail.

Having heard the chamberlain's announcement, the young fisherman did not bring that fish home but, instead, ran at once to the king's palace. When the guards saw the fish in his hand, they opened the gates.

The fisherman went in and was led to the king's throne room. There stood the chamberlain, his arms crossed before him and a great scowl upon his face. "Before I let you in, you must promise me one-half of your reward."

The fisherman was used to bargaining, because that was what happened at the market. "One-tenth," he said.

The chamberlain shook his head. Only commoners bargained. "One-half, and nothing less."

Well, there was little the fisherman could say to that. He could always take the fish home, but then he would get nothing at all. However, as he did not like the greedy chamberlain, he took a moment to think, and at last agreed.

The chamberlain smiled and opened the door. "Come in, come in."

When the fisherman entered the room carrying the big fish, the king clapped his hands in delight. "Wait here, good fisherman," he said, "and after my dinner you will have your reward."

A cook came out, took the fish, fried it up, and set it before the king. The king smacked his lips and gobbled the fish without using good manners, he was that hungry. But then, he was a king; he could act however he wished.

When he was done, he turned to the fisherman. "Now, my good young man, name your reward. Do you want gold? Rubies? A house in the country?"

The fisherman shook his head. "I want twenty lashes with your stick, Majesty."

The king was certain he had not heard correctly. "You want twenty gold pieces? Or twenty rubies?"

"No, sire," the fisherman said. "Just twenty lashes with your stick."

The king did not know what to do, which is unusual for a king. The fisherman had named his price. So he called over his servant. "Beat him softly, then."

The fisherman knelt. "No, my king. Hit me hard."

The king nodded reluctantly, and the servant began beating the fisherman.

After ten lashes, the fisherman leaped up. "Enough," he cried.

The servant looked puzzled.

The king looked puzzled.

The king did not like to look puzzled, though he did not mind it when his servants looked that way.

"The remaining ten lashes are your chamberlain's share," the fisherman said.

So the chamberlain was called in and forced to confess what he had done. Kneeling, he said, "But my lord, I asked for half of his reward. And this is half of his punishment."

"Reward or punishment—this is much too difficult for me," grumbled the king. He did not like things to be difficult, so he sent for his daughter, who was known as Princess Who Knows the Law.

The princess came quickly and listened to both sides. Then she said, "Father, the chamberlain and the fisherman were like partners in a business, the business of bringing a fish to your table. They agreed to share."

The king nodded, understanding. "Yes, yes..."

The princess smiled. "In a partnership, one must share the losses as well as the gains, the rewards as well as the—"

"Punishments!" the king cried. "Yes, yes, give the chamberlain ten very hard lashes with the cane." He clapped his hands.

"And then, Your Majesty," said the fisherman, "I should like to dissolve the partnership."

The princess laughed and spoke to the king. "I would remind you, Father, one of these men showed very good judgment in this case."

This her father understood at once. "The chamberlain will be dismissed from my service. Be a beggar or a thief for all I care. But be off. I will take the young fisherman as my chamberlain, for he has shown himself to be smart, quick-witted, loyal, and brave."

And so it was.

Jack and His Companions

A good friend is a hero, too

Once there was a poor widow in a land filled with poor widows, and she had one son named Jack.

It had been a harsh winter and a worse summer, and how they were to eat, neither she nor Jack knew.

"Mother, my own, I shall go out of this door this very night to seek my fortune. And if I find it, or it find me, I shall bring it home to you. You are my own dear mother, and no one deserves it more. So bake me a journeycake, and I'm away in the morning."

Well, the poor widow did as he asked, and in the morning she said to him, "Would you have half the cake and my blessing? Or would you have the whole and my curse?"

Jack shook his head. "Mother, my own, you know I would not have your curse for anything."

She smiled. "Then, my Jack, here's the whole with a thousand blessings besides." She watched till he was out of sight, then off she hurried to the church to light candles for his journey.

———

56

Jack went along and went along and went along, until he was that tired. He passed by the house of a farmer he knew well, and came to a bog where a poor donkey was up to his shoulders in mud.

"Ah, Jack, my boy, help me out or I will drown," called the donkey.

"Never ask twice, old donkey," Jack told him. He thought quickly, and threw stones and sod into the mire till there was good solid ground beneath the donkey. Then one step, two—and the donkey was saved.

"I am going along to seek my fortune," said Jack. "Seek it or find it, whichever comes first. Why not hump along with me?"

The donkey heed and then he hawed. "Why not, indeed. Two will make a greater fortune than one."

So they went along and went along and went along, and came upon a poor old dog, a kettle tied to his tail, and behind him a pack of boys taunting him.

"Help me!" cried the dog.

"Never ask twice, old dog," Jack told him. So he yelled and the donkey roared, and all those little gossoons turned and ran.

"Thank you, Jack," said the old dog as Jack untied the kettle from his tail. "Thank you, donkey."

"We are off to seek our fortune," said Jack. "Seek it or find it, whichever comes first. Why not hump along with us?"

The dog scratched one ear and then the other. "Why not, indeed. Three will make a greater fortune than two."

So they went along and went along and went along, until they stopped for the evening meal. Jack shared his journeycake with the dog, and the donkey ate grass by the roadside. Then, who should come by but a poor starving cat.

"May you never know a hungry belly," said the cat, eyeing their food. "And can I have a bite of that?"

"Never ask twice, old cat," Jack told him, and gave him the last bits of the bread to eat.

When the cat had finished his portion, and had cleaned himself from whiskers to tail, Jack said, "We are off to seek our fortune. Seek it or find it, whichever comes first. Why not hump along with us?"

The cat gave one more swipe at his whiskers. "Why not, indeed. Four will make a greater fortune than three."

So they went along and went along and went along, until they came upon a dark forest. They were about to go in when they heard a cackling cry. Just then a fox came trotting by, a fine black rooster in his mouth.

When the rooster saw Jack and his friends, he cried out, "Help me!"

"Never ask twice, old rooster," Jack told him, and before the words were out of his mouth, the dog took off after the fox. The donkey kicked at him, the cat clawed him, and the fox dropped the rooster and ran off.

When the rooster had unruffled his feathers and had gotten his coxcomb back to its full height, Jack said, "We are off to seek our fortune. Seek it or find it, whichever comes first. Why not hump along with us?"

"Why not, indeed," said the rooster, "for five will make a greater fortune than four."

So they went along and went along and went along, until they were deep into the forest with not a bit of light around them. The dark might have been frightening had not the cat and dog been able to see well in it and guide them all.

Then all of a sudden, the rooster began to crow. "Dawn!" he cried. "Dawn!"

"You silly bird," said the donkey. "It is nowhere near day."

Then Jack saw what the rooster had seen and pointed ahead. "Not dawn, but a bit of candlelight. And candlelight means a house. And a house means a bit of bedding. We are saved, my old companions."

So they shook themselves all over with happiness at the thought, and wading through brambles and briars, they headed toward the house.

But as they got closer, they heard singing and laughing and a great deal of cursing coming from the place.

"Better safe than sorry," said Jack.

"Better knowing than not," said the donkey.

"Better warned than whipped," said the dog.

"Better careful than caught," said the cat.

The rooster just flapped his wings, flew to one of the windows, peeked in, then flew back.

"Bad, my lads," he told the others. "Very bad indeed."

When they crept up and looked in, it was just as the rooster had said. Inside the house were six robbers. There were pistols and dirks and blunderbusses and cutlasses on the table. But on the table, too, were roast beef and pork, whiskey and mulled wine.

The robbers were laughing and swilling and talking with their mouths full.

"And didn't we gather a fine haul at Lord Dunlavin's?" said one robber.

"Gold and silver," said another.

"Silver and gold," said a third.

"And jewels for the counting!" said a fourth.

"And a fine lot of food," said the fifth.

The sixth robber smiled. "And all with the help of Lord Dunlavin's porter." He laughed.

The others laughed with him.

Outside, Jack whispered to his companions. "Here's my plan, old dears. Close ranks and listen."

Well, they listened and agreed and before you could say Jack-over-the-stile, the donkey put his forefeet on the windowsill. The dog climbed onto the donkey's head, the cat on the dog's head, the rooster on the cat's head.

Then Jack made a sign to them and they all began to sing out.

"Hee-haw, hee-haw!"

"Rouf-rouf-growl!"

"Meow-row-row!"

"Cock-a-doodle-do!"

"All up and over!" cried Jack. "No quarter and no half measures neither!"

They smashed that window, and then ran around smashing the others.

Well, didn't the robbers think that the king's troopers were on all sides? They blew out the candle and skedaddled and skelped out the back door and never looked behind.

So Jack and his companions got inside the house, closed the shutters, and ate up the food. Then they lay down to rest: Jack in the bed, the donkey in the hallway, the dog on the doormat, the cat by the fire, the rooster on a perch by the window. Soon they were all snoring, loud, soft, and in-between.

At first the robbers were relieved to find that no one had followed them. But the grass was damp, and they had nothing to eat. And all six of them thought about the treasures they had left behind.

The captain rubbed his beard. "I believe, my boys, that I will tiptoe back and see what I can see."

"That's why you are the captain . . . ," said one.

"And a fine captain, too," said another.

They all agreed.

So off he went, tiptoeing back to the cottage, where the shutters were closed and all the lights out, and the hearth fire nothing but embers.

The captain groped his way through the back door and toward the fire.

The cat rose up from his half-nap, which is how all cats sleep, and he came at the captain all teeth and claws.

The captain howled and yowled and ran to the front door, where the dog savaged him, arm, legs, and thigh.

The captain moaned and groaned and tried to get out of a window, and there the rooster dropped down on him, claws and bill.

The captain hooted and hollered, "Oh, tarnation and botheration," which was, in fact, the nicest thing he said—the rest I cannot tell you. Then he reeled into the hallway, where the donkey gave him a kick in the broadest part of his smallclothes, which landed him outside through the back door.

As for Jack, he was so tired, and the bed so soft, he never woke up, though he dreamed about setting things aright with Lord Dunlavin.

———

When the captain of the robbers got to his feet, dazed and wounded, he hurried back to his brethren.

"Well, any chance of getting back in?" they asked, for in the dark, they could scarcely see how badly he was hurt.

"Not a chance, not a chance," he cried. "For at the hearth fire lies an old woman with sharp claws. At the front door, a man with knives. At the window, some devil of an imp with sixpenny nails and awful wings. And in the hallway, some smith with a hammer who pelted me through the back door till I was black and blue and bloody. I'll not go back there for all of Lord Dunlavin's treasures. And if you are smart, you'll not go back either."

"Oh, captain," they cried, "we believe you." For the sun had come up even as he was telling his tale, and they could see how broken a man he was. So they ran off into another county and were never heard from again.

As for Jack and his companions, they got up with the dawn, made themselves a hearty breakfast, then put all the treasures in some knapsacks and saddlebags they found lying around. Then off they went to Lord Dunlavin's castle to give him back his treasures, for Jack had insisted on it. "Good fortune is one thing; a stolen treasure another," he said.

Who did they meet at the gate, airing his powdered head and showing off his white stockings and red breeches, but the very porter the robbers said had helped them.

"Go away, go away," said the porter, looking down his long nose at them. "No room here for the likes of you. Be off or I'll set the dogs on you."

"Aha!" said Jack, "But you set no dogs on the robbers last night. In fact, you invited them in, did you not?"

The porter's face got redder than his breeches. He sputtered and dribbled and houghed and snorted, but did not answer.

Now it happened that Lord Dunlavin and his pretty daughter were standing by their parlor window and overheard this whole exchange.

Lord Dunlavin put his head out the window. "I'll be glad, Mullins," he said, "to hear your answer."

"Ah, my lord, don't believe this rascal, for sure I didn't open the door to those six thieves. Not I," Mullins said.

"Who said a word about six?" said Lord Dunlavin.

"Aha!" Jack said. "You old rascal, we have you now. For six thieves there were. Didn't we come upon them in the woods and send them packing! And here, Lord Dunlavin, is all your gold and jewels. Though I must admit, the food got eaten up because we were starving after our battle with them."

"If it was you ate the food, it's but a first payment for the good deed you've done me," said Lord Dunlavin. "Come in, come in, and none of you will have a poor day from now till the time of your deaths."

"You see," said Jack to his comrades, "we have found our fortune!"

The donkey and the dog and the rooster got the best posts in Lord Dunlavin's farmyard. The cat got to live in the kitchen and get a daily bowl of cream.

Lord Dunlavin dressed Jack up like a gentleman, in frills and furbelows and a fob at his pocket, and made him the castle's steward.

Jack was so pleased with his lot, he sent for his old mother to live nearby, and they were all as happy as could be. All happy, that is, with the exception of Mullins, who was set out upon the road, Lord Dunlavin's dogs after him.

HUNGARY

The Truthful Shepherd

How truth and trickery together made a hero

Once there were two kings who were great friends: the king of Prussia, and Mátyás, the king of the Magyars. They met once a year and always drank a toast, one to the other.

This year when they met, the king of Prussia said, "Mátyás, my good friend, is it true that you own a sheep with a golden fleece?"

Mátyás nodded. "Yes, among my many flocks there is such a sheep. And among my many shepherds is one who is above the price of gold, for he is a man who never lies."

"Come, come, my friend," said the king of Prussia, "there is no such thing. Everyone lies, fibs, and prevaricates at some time or other."

"Not this young man," King Mátyás assured him.

The king of Prussia got red in the face. "I do not believe it."

"Then believe this," said King Mátyás, raising one finger. "Let us wager on my shepherd's truthful nature. If you catch him in a lie, I will give you half my kingdom."

The king of Prussia held out his hand. "I will take that wager, my dear old friend. And if he is truthful, I will give you half of mine."

64

So the two kings shook hands, and if you are thinking this is a silly thing for two rulers to wager on—lands, houses, farms, cities, and populations—it is at least better than going to war over it.

Now, the king of Prussia went right to his room and got into the clothes of a poor man: gray shirt, ripped trousers, and a tattered straw hat, though he kept his good shoes on, because he had a long ways to walk. Then off he went to the village where he had been told the truthful shepherd lived.

When he met the shepherd, the king doffed his hat. "Greetings, fair shepherd."

"Greetings to you, sire," said the shepherd.

The king of Prussia was taken aback. His mouth gaped open. "How did you know I was a king?"

"By the soft cut of your hair, your handsome shoes, and how well you spoke to me," the truthful shepherd replied.

The king of Prussia nodded. The shepherd was certainly observant. But whether he would remain truthful was still to be seen.

"I have a desire for the sheep with a golden fleece," said the king. "If you will get it for me, I will give you six horses and a carriage in return." Indeed, in those days that was a princely sum. The shepherd could have lived in luxury for the rest of his life.

"I cannot and I will not, sire," the shepherd said, not bothering to disguise his rejection with kind words. "King Mátyás would have my head if I did so."

"*Seven* horses, then, *two* carriages, and a house in the country," said the king, who could easily afford them. Especially after he won the wager.

"Not even for your own palace, sire," said the shepherd. He bowed and went off whistling.

The king of Prussia was astonished and angry and—if truth be told, as ever it should—a bit worried as well. He went back to his lodgings, and there his beautiful daughter, Helga, consoled him.

"Do not worry so, Papa," she said, "for I am certain that what money could not buy, love can. Love can trick even the most constant of young men."

So when evening came, off she went with a trunk full of gold and a flask of golden wine.

"Shepherd," she said, smiling prettily at him, "will you give me the golden fleece?" She tousled his hair and winked. She gave him a kiss on both cheeks and on his brow.

He kissed her back, full on the lips.

"I cannot give the golden fleece to you for money," he said, "for a man with no head has nowhere to spend. But if you will marry me, I will get you the sheep." For he thought, *If I am married to a princess of Prussia, the king of the Magyars surely cannot cut off my head.*

"I will marry you this moment," she told him. "Only skin the sheep and eat the meat. I want only the fleece."

So he did as she asked, and the minute he gave her the fleece, she ran off home.

"And when will we be married?" the shepherd called after her.

"When the sun and moon dance together in the sky!" she cried over her shoulder—and then she was gone.

For a moment the shepherd was distraught. What could he tell his king? He knew he had to report that the golden sheep was missing. But how to tell him the truth?

Then he thought, *A trickster can be tricked in turn.* He had a daring plan.

When morning came, the shepherd walked to the palace, thinking about his plan. It was a trick—but it contained the truth, for he was ever truthful.

King Mátyás and the king of Prussia were sitting at the breakfast table, and with them was the king's beautiful daughter, Helga. She had just finished telling them how she had tricked the shepherd and gotten the fleece.

The three looked up when the shepherd entered.

"Greetings, shepherd," said King Mátyás. "Any news for me?"

"Only this, sire," the shepherd said. "I have traded the golden sheep for a black sheep."

"A black sheep? That is a lie!" roared the king of Prussia, already counting his half of the Magyar kingdom.

But King Mátyás knew better. He trusted his truthful shepherd. "And where might that black sheep be now?"

"She is sitting there, between you and the king of Prussia," said the shepherd, "her hands in her long dark hair."

The princess looked down, as if ashamed of her trick.

King Mátyás laughed. "You have told the truth," he said. "For that I will give you the half of the kingdom I have just won from my good friend here."

The king of Prussia laughed, too. "And I will add to that portion my daughter in marriage, seeing that you are already promised, one to the other."

"Papa!" cried his daughter, but she was secretly glad, remembering the kisses of the night before.

Outside, the sun and moon danced in the sky together.

And believe it or not, that is how a Magyar became a Prussian, how a shepherd became a prince, and how truth became the order of the day. And when the shepherd was finally king, he ruled with honesty and fairness all his life long.

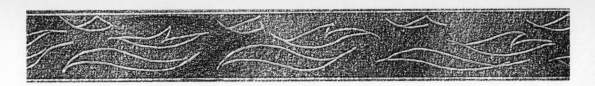

ISRAEL

And Who Cured the Princess?

Who gives the most gets the most

Once, in the long ago, there were three brothers who between them had not a single penny. So they decided to go out into the world. At a crossroads, they each took a separate path, vowing to meet back in ten years and share something remarkable.

The eldest brother went to the west, where the land was high and rough. He found work as a wizard's apprentice. He labored hard and never complained, and when the ten years were up, the wizard gave him a magic mirror that revealed everything going on in foreign lands.

"Use it wisely," the wizard cautioned.

The middle brother went to the east, where the land was low and lush. He found work as a sorcerer's apprentice. He labored hard and never complained, and when the ten years were up, the sorcerer gave him a magic carpet that could take him wherever he wished.

"Use it wisely," the sorcerer warned.

As for the youngest brother, he went south, where the land was rolling, and there he apprenticed to a gardener. He loved his work, and the gardener often told him he had magic in his hands. At the end of the ten years, the gardener gave him a magic apple that could heal the sick and dying.

"The apple is a miracle," said the gardener, "but no more than you, my boy. Take care of both."

So the brothers, each having won for himself something rare and wondrous, said farewell to their masters and rode off to meet at the crossroads where they had parted ten years before. There were tears, there were embraces. At last they showed off their gifts: the mirror, the carpet, and the apple.

"Let us see whose gift is the greatest," said the eldest brother as they sat under a date tree drinking their tea.

So he held up the mirror, and through it he could see far away. In the capital of their country was great consternation. The king's beautiful only daughter, Princess Arielle, lay deathly ill. Her father proclaimed that anyone who could cure her would have gold and jewels beyond counting.

"We can do this," the middle brother cried. "Come, climb on my carpet."

So the three brothers climbed aboard.

"Carpet," the middle brother said,

> *"Fly far, fly fast, and fly your best,*
> *Take us all without a rest."*

The carpet flew them to the capital city, where they went immediately to the palace and announced that they could cure the princess.

A guard took them into the throne room, where the king, looking old and ill himself, heard their claim.

"Be careful what you promise," the king told them, for he had had enough of charlatans and fools, of physicians and magicians who had promised much and delivered nothing. "If you do not cure my dear daughter, I shall have you hanged."

The brothers looked at one another.

"However," the king continued, "if you succeed, one of you shall marry my daughter, if that is her wish, and rule after me, while the others will serve as his ministers."

"Done," the brothers said.

They were so quick and resolute in their reply that the king believed them at once, and so he had them brought into the sickroom.

The princess lay as still as stone on her great canopy bed. She was gray with illness, like a shadow of beauty, not beauty itself.

"We will save you, Princess Arielle," the youngest brother promised, and he took the apple from one pocket, a knife from the other.

The king's soldiers were immediately on their guard, but the youngest brother held knife and apple up.

"I will cut the apple into four quarters," he said, "for Princess Arielle is clearly not able to eat it all at once." He did what he said, and handed the knife to the king for safekeeping.

Then, kneeling by the bed, he gently but firmly fed the apple, a little at a time, to the princess.

After she ate the first quarter, she opened her eyes.

After the second, she sat up in bed.

After the third, she threw off her covers.

And upon eating the last quarter, she danced around the room.

The king was so overjoyed, he called the three brothers back to the throne room. "You have saved my daughter from certain death. I will gladly fulfill my promise to you. Gold and silver, as much as you can carry. And in addition, one of you can marry my daughter, if she so chooses."

The princess came into the room. No longer gray, she was bursting with health. "I do so choose, Papa," she said. "For I would not be standing here alive and happy were it not for these three brothers. I would marry the one who in truth cured me."

The eldest brother bowed. "If it were not for my magic mirror, princess, we would never have known about you, so all the other gifts would have been useless. *I* should be your husband."

Then the middle brother bowed. "If it were not for my magic carpet, princess, we would never have gotten here in time, so the other gifts would have been useless. *I* should be your husband."

The third brother bowed. "But truly, without the apple, all the other gifts would have been in vain. For you would have died whether we saw you in the mirror or not, whether we got here in time or not. However, I will not argue with my brothers, who are older and wiser than I."

So the king called his adviser to the throne room and laid out the puzzle before him. The adviser pulled on his long beard, scratched his ear, then asked the eldest brother, "Is your mirror broken or still in one piece?"

The eldest brother smiled. "Still in one piece, my lord."

Then the adviser turned to the middle brother. "Is the carpet worn through from its travels or in one piece?"

"Still in one piece, my lord."

Then the adviser turned to the youngest brother. "Is your apple still intact?"

"It is almost entirely gone, my lord," said the youngest brother. "But for stem, seed, and core. Still, I would not have it otherwise."

"In that case," the adviser said, "the prize goes to you, for you gave up all to save the princess."

The king, the princess, and the other two brothers agreed that it was a just decision. So the youngest brother and Princess Arielle were married, and the feasting went on for seven days and seven nights, till they were all thoroughly tired of it.

As for the two older brothers, they were made the king's advisers and were married to the king's nieces.

The youngest brother planted what remained of the apple—for, indeed, *something* did remain. He grew an orchard full of apples that kept all the people in the kingdom healthy.

And everyone, truly, lived happily ever after.

ENGLAND

The False Knight on the Road

A child can be a hero, too

A young boy—let us call him Jack—was on his way to school. He was still in short pants, so he could not have been more than eight or nine years old. And he carried his books bound up in a leather strap over his back.

As he walked along the road, Jack whistled, partly to keep himself amused and partly, it must be said, to warn away the Devil, or so the saying goes.

The day was pearly, an early spring morn. The sun was just up over the horizon. Jack was in no hurry. He had never been first to school, though he had never been last, either. A good boy, a clever boy, a brave boy. But still a boy.

On the road ahead stood a knight wearing armor, a bright sword at his side. His helm was down, disguising his face. The sun shone on him and he glistened. It was odd, indeed, because this was long after the time of knights in armor, but well before the time of moving pictures.

Jack was stunned. He stood amazed.

"Where are you going?" asked the knight.

"I'm going to school," said Jack. But he said it thoughtfully. He was not supposed to talk to strangers along the road. And what could be stranger than a knight in full armor?

"What is that on your back?" asked the knight.

Jack was more thoughtful still. He wondered at the question. Was the knight being polite? Or was he being silly? Was this something to be afraid of, or something to enjoy?

The sun smiled on. The knight gleamed more fully.

"They are my books," Jack said, answering the question.

The knight leaned forward. His armor creaked alarmingly. "And what is under your arm?"

Jack leaned away from him. "It is my lunch, both meat and cheese."

The knight took a step forward. Jack took a step back.

"I wish you were strung up on the tree," the knight said.

Now Jack was frightened. But he kept his wits. They played riddle games at school, and this sounded like a riddle. So he answered, "And a stout ladder under me."

The knight took a step back, and Jack let out a breath of relief.

Then the knight lifted his visor, and a stern face stared out at Jack, a face with a pointed beard and eyes the color of steel. "And the ladder would snap," the man said. He smiled.

Jack felt cold. What could he answer? "And *you* would fall down?" He was not sure of this answer. He was not sure this was a game.

The man was no longer smiling. He stepped forward again.

Jack looked down at the man's long legs. For a moment, it was as if he could see through the armor, and there—for a shimmering second—he thought he saw a hoof. But how could that be? A man would have a foot, not a hoof. He looked up. The man was a step closer.

"I wish you were on the sea," the man said.

Jack took a quick breath. "And a good boat under me."

The man came closer still. "And a hole bored in the wood."

There was a tail. Jack was sure of it. The man had a tail!

"And you drowned!" Jack cried.

One more step and the man would be able to reach out and touch him.

"I wish you in Hell," said the man, grinning.

"And you in Heaven with God and his angels!" Jack cried. It was the only thing he could think of.

The man put a hand to his face—he seemed to be burning all over, as if the sun had set him afire. "Not Heaven!" he cried. "Do not mention it or my old enemy!"

"Amen!" said Jack. "Amen." Then he turned on his heel and ran all the way to school, as if the Devil himself were after him. He was the first one in class and all his lessons remembered. When later he walked home, he said his prayers out loud and was comforted every step of the way.

AFGHANISTAN

Hired Hands

Light is light and fair is fair

Once two brothers—Abdul and Abdullah—lived together on a dry-as-dust farm. Both their mother and father had long since died, and the rains had failed to come the year before, so their crops could not grow. The two of them were so poor, they were down to their last bag of rice.

"Brother," the elder, Abdul, said, "I must leave and find work elsewhere. If I am successful, I will send a goodly portion of my wages home to you. That way, both of us will eat and perhaps our farm will once again prosper, as in the days of our father and our grandfather before him."

Without another word, he set off, leaving the younger brother, Abdullah, behind.

Now Abdul had not yet traveled a full day and night when he came to a farm where there was still wheat and barley in the barn. Rain had clearly fallen here, and the farm was prosperous.

He knocked on the farmhouse door. "Do you need any help?"

The farmer who opened the door looked at the boy, up and down and sideways besides, though he did not look him straight in the eye. "You look both strong and hale," he said. "You will do."

Abdul was pleased at the ease with which he had found work.

"But here are my conditions," the farmer said. He smiled, and it was not a nice smile. More a snake smile than a man smile. No teeth showed. "You must stay until the first cuckoo of spring calls. And if you shirk your work or become angry at any time, you will pay me a penalty of fifty pieces of gold."

"I do not have any such treasure," protested Abdul.

"Ah, then you will have to work for me for seven years with no wages at all."

"I am not sure...," Abdul began.

But the farmer leaned out of the door, interrupting him. "There's more. If, on the other hand, *I* should become angry or ill-tempered at any time, then I will pay *you* a thousand rubles."

"A thousand rubles!" Abdul's eyes opened wide. He knew he was a good worker and he was not easy to anger. "Agreed," he said, and put his mark to the farmer's contract.

The farmer put him up that night, and in the morning, he took the elder brother to a field that had been lying fallow. The old grass was thigh-high and waved in the wind.

"Here," said the farmer, handing him a scythe. "Mow as long as there is light."

So Abdul mowed for all he was worth, swinging the scythe to and fro, and never worrying about his aching back. He thought only about the thousand rubles and how it would save his own farm from ruin.

When the sun went down, he kept on mowing. But when night came on, he stopped.

Returning to the farmhouse, he knocked on the door, and again the farmer opened it. "What, back so soon? I said to mow as long as there is light."

"But the sun went down some time ago," said Abdul.

The farmer laughed. "The sun is down but the moon is up. Light is light."

"But... but..."

"You are not angry?" the farmer asked slyly.

"No, no!" Abdul said quickly.

"Or trying to shirk your work?"

"No, no, no!" Abdul answered. "Though if I could have some water and a bit of a rest..."

"Back to the field," said the farmer, and he slammed the door.

So back Abdul went and worked as long as the moon was up.

Then the moon set and the sun rose. Light was light. Abdul had reached the end of his strength. He dropped to the ground and fell fast asleep.

Just then the farmer arrived at the meadow. He poked the boy with his foot. "Up, you lazy beggar. The sun is high. I will have no shirkers on my farm." He kicked the boy again.

Exhausted, Abdul looked up and cried out, "Curse you and your field, your bread and your rubles. I am a boy, not a mule." He stood and walked off down the road.

"Curse me all you like," the farmer called after him. "It only proves your anger. You owe me fifty gold pieces or seven years' work. I have the contract to prove it. Wherever you go, do not go far. And return within two days or I will send the guards after you."

Abdul stumbled home. When he arrived, looking exhausted and haggard, with lines down his cheeks from weeping, his younger brother, Abdullah, rushed out to greet him.

"What has happened? You look terrible."

"I have been tricked by a terrible villain," Abdul said, and told the story of what had happened.

"Let me take your place," Abdullah replied. "To be forewarned is to be forearmed. I will go to see that scoundrel, and I will not say we are brothers. He will not find me so easily guiled."

The two embraced and ate the last of the rice, then off the younger brother went down the road.

———

He found the farm with ease and knocked on the door. The farmer agreed to take him on and offered him the same contract with the same conditions.

"Oh, no," said Abdullah, "that is much too small. Let us make it a hundred gold pieces or fourteen years of work without pay should I shirk my duties or get angry. And two thousand rubles should you get angry first. All to be done by the time the first cuckoo of spring calls."

"Done!" said the farmer, who had played this trick many times before.

So Abdullah got a good meal at the farmer's expense and a soft bed for the night.

In the morning, the farmer was up with the dawn, ready to show his latest dupe the meadow.

The sun got higher and higher and the farmer grew more and more impatient. At last he went to Abdullah's door, knocked, and walked in.

"The sun is high. Light is light, and you lie abed dreaming," the farmer said roughly. "I expect you think grass mows itself."

Abdullah looked up sleepily. "Are you angry?" he asked.

The farmer caught himself in time and answered in a gentler voice, "No, no. Not angry. Not the least bit angry. Only... only I wanted to remind you that your work awaits."

"Ah," Abdullah said, and smiled sweetly, "then I will get dressed." And as the farmer watched, he pulled on his pants slowly, brushing off pieces of grass and lint that only he could see. Then he shook his shirt out and pressed it between his hands, humming as he did so. Then he put on his boots, changing the laces from right boot to left, so that they should wear down evenly. Finally, he took out his comb and went through his sleep-tangled hair with care.

All this took many minutes, of course, and the farmer began to get uneasy. "Hurry up, lad. Though I can wait, the meadow cannot."

Abdullah smiled that sweet smile again. "Are you getting angry, master?"

The farmer caught himself in time. "No. No. Not at all." But on his forehead grew lines as deep as furrows.

At last Abdullah was fully dressed, and he accompanied the farmer to the meadow, where the other farmhands were eating their lunch.

"Ah," Abdullah said, "lunch first, work after. I will be like the others."

The farmer could not very well refuse without showing his anger, and—as one might have guessed—the boy was a slow eater, chewing everything not once but two and three times over.

"My mother said I should," Abdullah confided, "and one must always listen to one's mother."

"Yes, yes," the farmer said, but his fingers were beginning to drum against his thighs. The furrows on his brow were now deep enough for planting.

Abdullah finally finished eating, but before the farmer could urge him to the field, he said, "And my mother always reminded me that a nap after such a good meal is a must. Otherwise one cannot work to one's capacity."

"No nap! No nap!" the farmer cried.

"Not angry, sir?" asked Abdullah. "After all, you said one should listen to one's mother."

"Not . . . angry!" shouted the farmer. Then more softly, he said, "Not at all."

Abdullah lay down and was soon snoring away, and he slept until the sun went down and the moon came up.

The farmer was beside himself. He shook his fist at the boy. He stamped his feet. "Get up!" he shouted. "The day is gone. The night is come. Wake up."

But Abdullah kept on snoring.

The farmer foamed at the mouth. "May the one who sent you here fall down the stairs and break his neck!"

Abdullah opened his eyes.

"My, my, sir—I had a strange dream and in it you were shouting. Are you angry with me?"

"No, no. I only wanted to say that it's dark and . . ."

"Ah, dark—then we'd best get back for dinner," Abdullah said, and he pulled the astonished farmer toward the house.

When they got there, the farmer's wife announced, "Husband, we have two visitors." She nodded to two fine gentlemen waiting in the kitchen. "I have invited them to dinner but have not yet made the meal."

The farmer turned to the boy and said, "Go and slaughter a chicken for our dinner."

Abdullah nodded. "Of course, sir, but which?"

"Any you find on the path," said the farmer.

"And which path?" asked Abdullah.

"The one we just came on," the farmer replied.

So off went Abdullah.

But before he could return, the farmer's neighbors came running to the house. They were shouting, "Quick! Quick! Come out!"

The farmer went outside to see what was the matter, and a man called to him, "Your farmhand has gone mad. He has slaughtered your entire flock of hens and the rooster as well."

The farmer tore his hair. What could this mean? He rushed up the path to find Abdullah surrounded by blood and feathers.

"You idiot!" he cried. "What have you done?"

"Why, what you asked me to do, master," said Abdullah. "You told me to slaughter any chicken I found on the path and here they all were!" He looked up and smiled sweetly. "Are you angry with me?"

Angry? The farmer was furious, but he did not dare say so. "No...," he declared through clenched teeth. "But it is a pity my entire flock is gone."

And so things went for a month, one disaster after another, until the farmer was all but ruined.

The farmer was beside himself. He could barely contain his anger. So he began to plot and plan for a way out of his contract without having to pay the two thousand rubles. Bad enough he owed the boy at all. His one hope was that spring was near and soon the first cuckoo would call.

"Perhaps I can speed the bird up," he decided. So he told his wife his plan.

Soon the wife was up a tree and the farmer had invited the boy to go hunting with him.

"But, master," said Abdullah, "I do not know how to handle a bow."

"You will learn. You will learn," promised the farmer, and led him under the very tree where his wife waited.

As soon as she saw them, she began to sing like a bird, "Cuckoo! Cuckoo!"

"My, my," said the farmer, "spring here already? That is the first cuckoo. My boy, you are free to go home."

But Abdullah was wise to the old farmer and had been waiting for just such a trick. "It is still winter, master, too soon to be a cuckoo. But I have heard that there is a squirrel who can sing just like a bird, and often fools the listeners. Squirrels make such good eating, master. I will practice my hunting and bag us a squirrel for supper." He raised the bow and aimed it at the tree, pretending he was ready to shoot.

"No! No!" the farmer cried, and flung himself on the boy.

"But how else I am to learn to hunt?" Abdullah asked, getting up and aiming the bow once again. He pulled the bowstring back.

The farmer was so undone, he failed to notice that there was no arrow nocked in the bow. He began screaming, "Go away from here, you idiot, you ignoramus, you fool!"

"Why," the boy said with a great smile on his face, "I think, master, that you are angry."

"Angry?" the farmer said, shaking with rage. "I am *furious*! You have done hardly a speck of work all month, you have slaughtered all my chickens, and now you would murder my wife. Get out, get away. It's worth the money to be rid of you."

By this time, they were surrounded by the farmhands, all of whom had been tricked by the farmer. They cheered and cheered.

The farmer's wife came out of the tree with no help from anyone.

The farmer went back to the house, and from a secret hiding place, he took out two thousand rubles. He flung them at Abdullah's feet. "There! Go!"

"Not until you tear up my contract and those of all these good workers." Then Abdullah paid the farmer what each hired hand—and his brother— owed. Even with that, he had many rubles to spare.

The farmhands hoisted Abdullah to their shoulders and walked him all the way home, where his brother came out and greeted him with many embraces.

As for the farmer, he had learned his lesson, and never again did he trick anyone into working on his farm, but paid a just wage. To his surprise, many of his old farmhands came back to work for him, and they worked harder than they had ever done before.

So everyone prospered: the farmer and his wife; the farmhands and their families; and not the least, the two brothers, Abdul and Abdullah. For with their rubles, they were able to buy good seed, to dig a well so deep it never ran dry, and to live quite happily—with hard work—ever after.

FINLAND

Mighty Mikko

*Who can withstand a brave heart,
a strong faith, and a sly friend?*

Once, long ago, when the world was still filled with magic, an old woodsman and his wife had a single son named Mikko. For many years, they were happy together, there in the great woods. But one day, alas and alack, the mother took ill and died. Soon after that, the father died, too, from a heart left uncomforted.

However, before he died, the old woodsman called his son to him. "I have nothing to leave you, my dear Mikko, but three snares. When I am dead, go into the woods and if you find a wild creature in any of those snares, free it carefully and take it home to live with you."

"Father, do not die," Mikko cried. But it was too late.

As soon as he had buried his father by his mother's side, and had wiped his face of the rainfall of tears, Mikko remembered the snares. He went out to the woods and searched for them.

The first two were empty, but in the third was a little red fox, whimpering at its fate.

Carefully, Mikko opened the trap, then he carried the fox home in his arms. He fed it the scraps he had planned to eat for his own supper. And when he went to sleep that night, with an empty stomach but a full heart, Mikko felt the little fox curl up at his feet.

It was the first time, but not the last, because the two became companions and lived together for many days. Mikko planted wheat for bread and beans for the pot. The fox brought home rabbits for the stew. They should have been happy, but Mikko was not.

"I am lonely," he told the fox.

"You have me," the fox replied. Of course he replied—this was in the days of magic, remember?

"You are a fox and I am a young man," said Mikko. "It is not enough."

The fox smiled. His teeth were very white and very sharp. "Then marry, Mikko."

"Alas and alack," Mikko replied, his head in his hands, "I am too poor to marry."

"Balderdash!" said the fox. "You are a handsome young man, and better still, you are a gentle and kind companion. Even the princess could do no better."

"The princess!" Mikko looked up, and for the first time in many days he began to laugh. "I will marry the princess when pigs can fly."

"You do not want to marry the princess?" the fox asked, looking at Mikko through the corner of his right eye. You must remember that foxes are *very* sly.

"I would marry the princess in an instant if she would have me," said Mikko. "But look around you, fox. I am a poor man in a poor house with a poor field full of poor wheat and poor beans. No princess would marry me. No poor girl, either." He put his head back in his hands.

"Leave it to me," said the fox. "Be brave. Have faith. Do as I tell you, and you will be a happy master. I will arrange the wedding."

Mikko put his hand over his heart. "I will be brave and have faith," he said. Then, before Mikko could stop the fox, the little creature trotted off to have an audience with the king.

———

The fox bowed low before the king. "My master, Mighty Mikko, sends you greetings."

The king was not astonished that the fox could talk. This was back in the days of magic, remember? But he did not want to admit that he did not know this Mighty Mikko, for that would mean that he was stupid or forgetful, two things kings should never be, but, alas, too often are.

"You know Mighty Mikko, of course," said the fox. "He who slew the great army of Novgorod and drained Lake Saimaa in a single swallow."

"Of course," the king said, "Mighty Mikko, my old friend. How is he?"

"He is off on a journey and requests that you send him a bushel measure," said the fox.

"Anything for Mikko," said the king, and he ordered that the bushel measure be brought at once from the storeroom.

The fox bowed again when he took the measure, and off he went into the woods, where he hid it in a hollow tree that only he knew about.

Then back he went to the nearby town, and sniffed about the farm acreage till he found where the farmers had buried their treasures. He took a gold piece from one, a silver from another, a copper from a third, and so on, until he had more than a pawful. These he brought back and stuck in various cracks in the measure. Then he returned the very next day with the measure and gave it back to the king.

Bowing low once more, the fox said, "Oh, king. My master, Mighty Mikko, thanks you for the use of your measure."

The king smiled and took the measure from the fox. Then he peeped in, trying hard not to seem greedy, which is difficult for kings, I know. He wanted to see what the measure had been used to count. He had forgotten that foxes are sly. And, of course, he spied the gold and silver and copper lodged in the cracks.

Only a very rich man, the king thought, *would be so careless with his coins.* "I should like to meet your master again," said the king.

Pretending that this was never his intention at all, the fox bowed again. "Alas and alack," he said, his voice dripping with sincerity, "my master is about to embark on a long journey. He wishes to be married and must meet a dozen foreign princesses who are being offered up for his inspection." For that, of course, was the way things used to be back in the days when kings and rich men bought wives instead of wooing them.

Of course, this made the king even more eager to have Mikko come for a visit. *Perhaps,* he thought, *Mikko will like my daughter best.* So he said to the fox, "No, no, dear Sir Fox, but I insist that your master come here first. I . . . I would like to talk over old times with him before he goes on his long journey."

The fox rubbed his right ear with his paw and managed to look embarrassed. "Ah, Your Majesty, I would love to suggest this to him. But—well, you see, it is like this . . ." And he leaned over to whisper into the king's ear. "You are actually not rich enough to entertain my master, and your castle is not big enough to house all the retainers who always travel with him. He is not called Mighty Mikko for nothing, you know."

By now, of course, the king was more than eager—indeed, *frantic* would be a better word—to meet with Mikko. He had totally forgotten that foxes are sly. "I will give you anything, fox, if you can persuade your master to stop by here."

The fox shook his head.

"Why not a smaller retinue for a quick side trip?"

The fox shook his head again, but a bit slower this time.

"Is there nothing I can do to . . ."

The fox smiled. "Mighty Mikko would never travel with less than his full company," said the fox. "But sometimes—as a prank—he likes to go about disguised as a poor woodsman, with me as his only attendant."

The king leaped up, clapping his hands. "Oh, dear Sir Fox, let him come that way. And once he is here, I will have a wardrobe ready for him, and chambers fit for a king."

Well, they argued and bartered and traded for a good five hours, till at last the fox got the king to promise to have ready the very finest silken breeches, the very best embroidered coat, leather boots with a high polish and silver buckles, and a hat the color of old plums with a feather that stood half a hand's-span high.

"That may just do," said the fox. "I shall endeavor to bring Mighty Mikko tomorrow." And off he went.

The next day, the fox came back with the handsome young Mikko by his side.

"How am I to act at a palace?" asked Mikko.

"Be brave. Have faith. Do as I tell you, and you will be a happy master," the fox replied.

Mikko put his hand over his heart. "I will be brave and have faith," he said.

The fox smiled. "Furthermore, always answer every question with another, and always laugh at the princess's jokes."

The princess had been warned by her father to be on her very best behavior, but when she peeped out of the window and saw Mikko, she sighed. Turning to her lady-in-waiting, she said, "I think I could love him even were he only a poor woodsman."

The lady-in-waiting sighed back. "My princess, it is easier to love a rich man than a poor one. Or so my father always told me."

And they laughed behind their hands, which is what ladies of fashion have always done.

An hour later, when she was all dressed and ready, the princess went down the stairs to have tea with her father and his guests.

Mikko was now dressed in the king's coat and breeches, with the high-polished, silver-buckled boots that reached up to his thighs. The plum-colored hat with its long feather was at his side.

The princess looked at Mikko for a long time without speaking.

"Your Highness," the fox said to the princess, "this is Mighty Mikko."

"I see you are better dressed now, sir," the princess said. "Do you prefer these clothes to your others?"

Remembering the fox's advice, Mikko answered, "Should I not?"

"Surely they are softer than the woodsman's garb, though you are no different in them." She smiled.

Mikko leaned back and laughed heartily.

This, the princess thought, *is the man I shall marry.* Then she blushed prettily because she knew, even if no one else did, that she had fallen in love with him.

The fox knew. He could smell love on her. And he grinned.

The next day, the fox returned alone to the palace and spoke to the king. "Mighty Mikko is a man of quick and thorough judgment, and he begs me to ask for your daughter's hand."

"My good fox," said the king, who flapped his hands around as if he could not think what to say next.

"Consider carefully, Majesty," said the fox. "My master would have your decision tomorrow. It is not for nothing he is called Mighty Mikko."

"I . . . I will give you my decision today," said the king. "Right now, in fact. Let them be married, I say. There is no one I would like better for a son-in-law than Mighty Mikko."

So in a day they were engaged, and in another, married. But after the ceremony, Mikko took the fox aside.

"Now that I am married, fox, what am I to do?" asked Mikko. "I cannot remain here at the king's palace with my wife forever."

"Be brave."

"I am afraid, fox," said Mikko.

"Have faith," the fox said.

"That is harder and harder," said Mikko.

"Do as I tell you," said the fox, "and you will be a happy master."

Mikko sighed, but he put his hand over his heart. "I will be brave and have faith," he said.

The fox smiled. "Tonight, tell the king, your new father, that he should visit you next in your own castle, over which his daughter shall rule."

"But I have no castle," said Mikko.

"By tomorrow you shall," the fox said, "and this is how it will go. You shall start off at first light and travel north till you come to a crossroads. Turn left till you see the towers of a great castle, and head for it. Whatever men and women you see in the fields, ask them whose people they are, and do not be surprised at their answer."

"But, fox...," said Mikko.

"What about having faith?" asked the fox. "What about being brave? Have I not gotten you fine clothes? Have I not gotten you married to a princess? The rest will be no harder." And off he went.

Well, the fox disappeared down the road, and at the crossroads, he turned left. Soon he came upon a dozen woodsmen with axes over their backs.

"Good day, kind cutters," said the fox, "and whose men are you?"

"Our master is a wicked old dragon," they said.

The fox shook his head and looked aghast. "Poor men. Do you not know that the king is coming with a powerful army to destroy the dragon and all his people?"

The woodsmen trembled and muttered and looked quite ill. Finally, one of them said, "How can we escape?"

The fox put a paw to his head as if he were thinking great thoughts. At last he said, "Well, here's my idea. If you told the king that you were Mighty Mikko's men, he would spare you, I know, for Mighty Mikko has just married his daughter."

The fox went a little farther down the road and met two dozen grooms leading two dozen horses. They, too, were appalled when they heard of the approaching army. And they, too, promised to name themselves "Mighty Mikko's men" when the king asked.

The same happened with the shepherds, the reapers, the gardeners, and the milkmaids. All were happy to know they could be spared.

———

At last the fox trotted up the pathway to the castle itself. Inside lay the dragon, curled up around a pile of gold and jewels he had stolen. He yawned and showed yellow teeth to the noonday sun.

Once upon a time, this dragon had been a mighty creature and had stolen a castle and all its servants away from a good and honest prince, killing him in battle. But the dragon had grown fat and fatuous and lazy. He had become bloated and bigheaded and a brag.

The fox pretended to be awed by the dragon. "Are you famous?" he asked.

The dragon preened. "I am," he said, belching a little bit of smoke. "I am also great and wicked."

The fox pretended to be frightened. "Then I am sorry for you, truly I am."

"Sorry for me?" The dragon drew himself up. And up. And up. He was a very big dragon, even if somewhat fat and bloated. "Sorry for ME!"

"Why, you do not know the king is coming with a great force to destroy you and all your people?" asked the fox.

The dragon was the one to look frightened now. He knew he was fat and fatuous and lazy. He knew he had become bloated and bigheaded and a brag. But as long as his reputation had preceded him, there had been nothing to worry about. As long as people were frightened of him, no one had dared to challenge him.

Till now.

"When is this king coming?" he squeaked.

"Why," said the fox, "he is on the road now." The fox looked over his shoulder. "And he brings destruction in his path, which is why I am running off myself. I suggest you do, too."

The dragon gulped a bloated gulp and agreed. "I shall pack my belongings and go at once."

The fox shook his head. "You are too fat to run far, and I doubt those wings could lift your gargantuanness."

"Then what should I do?" asked the fat dragon.

"Hide yourself in the shed where the fireworks are kept," said the fox.

"Yes, yes," said the dragon. "The king will never find me there."

Dragons are big. And many are dangerous. No one ever said that dragons are smart. The fox counted on that.

So the fat, wicked old dragon hid in the shed, under the firecrackers, sparklers, spinners, and wheels. The fox locked the door behind him. Then he set fire to the shed. And *pow! whizz! zzzzz! bam!* Soon there was nothing left of that dragon except hot ashes.

Meanwhile, Mikko and his new wife and his new father-in-law, along with all the men and women and children of the kingdom, were coming down the road admiring the far-off fireworks.

"Oh, my dear," said the princess, "did you set those off for me?"

"Who else?" said Mikko, answering her with a question.

When they came to the crossroads, they turned left. After a while, they came to the woodsmen.

"Whose woodsmen are you?" asked the king.

Frightened, the woodsmen cried out, "We are Mighty Mikko's men."

Mikko was surprised, but he said nothing, and everyone was impressed with his modesty.

On and on the king and his people went, and they came to the grooms with the horses.

The king asked, "Whose grooms are you?"

The grooms cried out so loud, the horses trembled. "We are Mighty Mikko's men."

The shepherds said the same, as did the reapers, the gardeners, and the milkmaids.

The king was impressed, and so were his people. And when they got to the castle, they were greeted by the fox, and behind him all the guards and all the servants. "We are Mighty Mikko's people," said the guards and servants, "and we have a mighty meal prepared for you."

———

The king stayed on for several days, until they were all quite tired of feasting. So the king turned to Mikko. "It is time I went home, though my castle will seem dull and small now that I have visited yours."

"Oh, no," said Mikko, "when I first came to your castle, I thought it the most beautiful in the world." He spoke with such sincerity, the king knew at once that he did not lie.

So the king and his people returned home, satisfied that the princess had gained the perfect husband. And the princess remained in the old dragon's castle with the knowledge that she had married the man she loved.

As for the fox, he returned to the woods. "For I have paid you back, dear Mikko, for saving my life. We are quits now, you and I."

Mikko was sad to see him go. "I owe everything to you," he called after the fox.

The fox turned and grinned. "Not I!"

Mikko thought about that until the fox's red plume of a tail disappeared down the road. Then he understood: Really, he had his own father to thank for his good fortune, for his father had left him the snares that caught the fox. And he had his own good heart to thank, for *he* had rescued the fox from the snares.

An Open Letter
to Nana

You said we needed this book, and we do. Not to remind ourselves that boys can be heroes. We already knew that. They are in every movie and TV show and book and computer game, romping and stomping on the villains, using knives and guns and howitzers and ninja moves.

No, we need this book to remind us that there are other ways to be heroes. That heroes can use cleverness instead of cleavers. That a hero needs wits as well as will. Bravery takes brains—and you have shown us this in these stories.

And we need this book because these great stories have to be shaken out every so often, like some old camp blanket that's been stored away all year. If they are not told, they will die.

But girls need to read these tales, too. Because while *we* know boys using brainpower instead of firepower can be heroes, girls need to know it as well.

Your loving sons and grandson

Notes on the Stories

"THE MAGIC BROCADE"

This popular folktale from southern China has been made into a children's picture book at least three separate times in the past twenty-five years. It lends itself wonderfully to illustration.

I have blended several versions, giving my weaver's sons traditional names garnered from other Chinese folktales, and have spent more time on the youngest son's adventures than on those of the older two.

I especially like the incident of the hero knocking out his own front teeth. It is a particular kind of self-sacrifice one does not often see in folk stories.

Unlike many similar European stories of three brothers who go off to seek help for their parents—where the lazy ones end up either forgiven or torn to pieces—this tale ends on a note of some particular justice, as the two older brothers are left beggars. (This is in the original story and I have not tampered with it.) Interesting to note is that the older brothers are so shamed here, they do not even stay around to try to cadge from their own mother and brother's good fortune.

I hope you noticed that like Dorothy in Oz, Wang Xing gets home by clicking his magical shoes. This, too, is in the original tale.

"THE YOUNG MAN PROTECTED BY THE RIVER"

This Angolan story comes from a literal English translation of a tale in the Make dialect, first set down in 1894. The original translation is very spare. For example, the story begins this way: "A young man was given as a pledge by his uncle, the pledge of an ox."

While this tale may seem at first to be a simple rags-to-riches story, it certainly has the unlikely hero motif. The Lukala River plays an interesting role in the story. As the nineteenth-century translator says in his notes, the river "acts the part of just Providence, by rescuing an innocent slave from his bondage, and enriching him above his countrymen."

In the original story, there are simply the three baskets filled with guns/cloth/

medicines, with no thought as to how they might be used. I have expanded on that because it is central to the character of Kingungu (a name I took from another Angolan story, by the way, because the boy is not named in the original text) and central to his choice. It is what makes him a hero. He chooses *not* to use the guns or cloth as a means to free himself from slavery.

I have also added the various diseases that, research tells me, often are found in Angola.

I have kept one thing that may seem odd to a western ear: the traditional ending, where the storyteller recites three sayings, all of which mean "I am finished." Other countries have different kinds of closings—for example, Europeans say, "They all lived happily ever after."

"THE DEVIL WITH THE THREE GOLDEN HAIRS"

This popular story is number 29 in the Brothers Grimm collection, tale type 461 crossed with type 930, the rich man and his son-in-law. More than three hundred versions have been found in Europe alone. It has also made its way to China and Africa, and there is a version told by the Thompson River Indians of British Columbia and another told by a Portuguese community in eastern Massachusetts.

The story of a boy carrying a letter that says he is to be killed goes back to the Greek myths, where Bellerophon carried such a letter to a king. In fact, the term *Bellerophonic letters*, meaning any kind of communication that a person carries that contains information prejudicial to himself, arose from that story.

In my telling, I have made a repeating refrain of *child of good fortune*, and of the boy calling the two old women madam, which makes them want to help him. In the original, the Devil's grandmother delouses him, meaning she picks lice out of his hair, but that is such a bizarre concept to modern readers that I have changed it. I have also added the bits about giving the gold-laden donkeys to the miller and his wife, and ruling the kingdom afterward with good fortune, because those two things seemed to me to be implicit in the tale.

Otherwise—except for putting the story in my own words—I have followed the plot of the Grimm tale closely.

"EATING WITH TROLLS"

The basic story comes from the famous 1845 collection *Norwegian Folk Tales*, edited by early folklorists Peter Christen Asbjørnsen and Jørgen Moe. In that collection, the story is called "The Lad Who Had an Eating Match with the Troll." It is one of the most popular of the Norwegian tales (also known as *eventyr*), and there is hardly a collection from the region that does not include a variation. Askeladden, or Ash Lad, is a popular hero, and he stars in many other stories. He is a kind of Jack figure who defeats giants and trolls, makes a princess laugh, and has grand adventures.

As with many of the Norwegian tales, this one is centered around the family farm. The troll is a traditional folk character in that countryside—big, powerful, dangerous, and stupid.

The story was popular not just in Norway. Two of its three elements—throwing the stone and squeezing the stone—can be found elsewhere. In "Brave Tailor" (or "Stupid Ogre") story sequences, the throwing motif (type 1062) and the squeezing motif (type 1060) are found in northern Europe and have been carried to Africa, America, and the Philippines. The cheese incident goes way back to the Indian *Panchatantra*. It has found its way into several hundred versions of this tale, not only in Europe but in Indonesia and the Americas as well.

The eating contest motif (type 1088) is found throughout northern Europe and among Native Americans, though it is not clear whether the eating contest stories traveled there or were independently invented. And the motif in which the enterprising young hero tells the troll (or ogre or giant) that he will bring in the entire well of water (type 1049) is also popular and known throughout northern Europe.

One of the bloodiest of the variant stories is from North Carolina, a Jack tale called "Jack and the Giants' New Ground" found in *Folklore on the American Land* as well as in Richard Chase's *Jack Tales* and Joanna Cole's *Best-Loved Folktales of the World*.

For my retelling, I started with the Norwegian story, added the bird-throwing incident, gave the characters more dialogue to flesh them out, described the troll, made the troll's blunt "Stop chopping in my forest or I will kill you" a bit more engaging by putting it in a rhyme, and rearranged the timing of the placement of the knapsack.

"KNEE-HIGH MAN"

Many different stories of Knee-High Man are popular throughout African American folklore. A basic version of this particular tale can be found in Roger D. Abrahams's *Afro-American Folktales*. Dialect versions are included in *The Book of Negro Folklore*, edited by Langston Hughes and Arna Bontemps, and in Carl Carmer's *Stars Fell on Alabama*.

I have taken that basic story, given each character a bit more action, characterized Knee-High Man's little voice, and modernized the language somewhat.

"LANGUAGE OF THE BIRDS"

I found the basic story in Leonard A. Magnus's *Russian Folk-Tales,* a volume published in 1915. A Mayan version tells the same story, except that the boy in it is the son of a farm laborer, there is no nightingale, and there are four crows, not three. In that version, the judgment is that the boy crow goes with his father, the girl crow with her mother.

There are, of course, many stories throughout the world in which a young hero learns the language of birds and animals. However, the thrust of this tale is never the learning of the language, but what the hero does with the knowledge.

In my retelling, I have made several full scenes from the original's straight narrative. I have given Vasili more of a personality than he has in the old tale, but I have stuck close to the plot of the original Russian version.

"THICK-HEAD"

This Abenaki story is related to a type of story that folklorists call "The Profitable Exchange" (type 1655), in which a man who owns only one piece of corn that is eaten by a rooster gets to keep the rooster, then a hog that eats the rooster, then an ox that eats the hog. Stories of this type have been discovered around the world, from Europe, including the British Isles, to the Philippines. The particular Abenaki tribe from which this story was collected came from Canada, so they could have had many opportunities to trade stories—as well as furs—with French voyageurs.

The Abenaki lived for centuries in areas of Vermont, New Hampshire, and Maine, where they were called people of the dawnland because they dwelled on the east coast, where the sun rose first. In the seventeenth and eighteenth centuries, the Abenaki were pushed north into Canada by the English colonists.

I have taken the rather bare-bones original story and fleshed it out. In the original tale, Thick-Head kills both the fox and the wolf.

"THE FISHERMAN AND THE CHAMBERLAIN"

This Burmese tale (type 1610) is quite common in northern and eastern Europe, and has been recorded in Spain and India as well. According to Stith Thompson in *The Folktale,* it may have actually begun its life not as a folktale but as a medieval or Renaissance literary anecdote; a particular type of tale known as "The Deceptive Bargain" was extremely popular in medieval jest books.

I have followed the Burmese plot carefully but, of course, have added my own dialogue and pointed comments about kings and commoners.

"JACK AND HIS COMPANIONS"

Clearly, this story is a variant of the Brothers Grimm tale "The Bremen Town Musicians" (tale 27). Its earliest publication was in the 1866 book *Legendary Fictions of the Irish Celts* by Patrick Kennedy, whom Joseph Jacobs called "the Irish Grimm." A Dublin bookseller, Kennedy collected many Irish tales over a short period of time (1866–1871).

In this story, Jack is a formidable organizer and planner, but when it comes to the actual routing of the robbers, he leaves the work to his companions. I love that Jack does not marry Lord Dunlavin's daughter, though he does, indeed, rise up from his previous lowly position. Most important, he does not forget his mother, whose many blessings on his behalf surely had much to do with her son's good fortune.

I have taken out some of the most egregious Irishisms, which sound more like an Englishman's vision of a stage Irishman, and have made, instead, a kind of lilting tale-telling.

"THE TRUTHFUL SHEPHERD"

I came upon this version of this story in *Magyar Tales,* from the University of Massachusetts, but the story has been popular in Hungary since the sixteenth century, at least. In fact, King Mátyás—who was a real king of Hungary (1443–1490), known for his justice and humanity—is one of the most popular figures in the Hungarian folk tradition. Almost immediately after his death, legends and stories collected around him, just as happened with Arthur of Britain and Charlemagne of France. Stories about him are told in Hungary to this day.

The way I tell the tale shortens considerably the time the shepherd worries about what to report to the king and lengthens considerably what happens between the shepherd and the princess. After all, they are to be married!

I added the sun and the moon dancing together, because I believe that all eclipses—though scientifically explainable—are magical at the core.

"AND WHO CURED THE PRINCESS?"

My retelling is very loosely based on an Israeli version of the tale found in *Folktales of Israel,* but, in fact, the motif of princess given to man who can heal her (motif H346) has been found all over the world. The parent tale is called "The Four Skillful Brothers," and fourteen variants are found in Turkey alone. There is even an interesting—if brief—retelling in dialect in the Sea Islands of South Carolina called "Trackwell, Divewell, Breathewell," in which Breavewell [sic] says, "All for that which you folk have done, the woman is mine, because she was dead, an' I brought life into her again." In the old Hindu collection *Vetalapanchauinsati (Twenty-Two Tales of a Demon)*, there is a similar story. *The Five Chinese Brothers,* a rather well-known children's book beloved in the mid–twentieth century, is the same basic story.

According to folklore scholar Jack Zipes, "The first European literary version of this tale type was written in Latin by Girolamo Morlini, and Straparola translated it and adapted it." The story thus entered European consciousness and ended up in multiple versions across the continent and in the Grimms' collection as "The Four Skillful Brothers."

The idea of something magical that can heal—healing waters, fruits, and the like—is always popular and has found its way into many different kinds of stories, often ones in which the older brothers, in anger, somehow hurt the younger and take away his magical gift. But this particular story almost always has a happy ending, though the princess is not always the prize. In the Grimm version, for example, the king decides this way: "Since it would be impossible to give the maiden to each of you, no one shall have her. Nevertheless I shall reward you with half my kingdom to be divided among the four of you." And in the Chilean version, "The Five Brothers," the king luckily has five daughters, "and each of them is going to marry one of you boys." It finishes, "That was the end of the squabble. The king himself married them all, baptized them, and gave the five true men his blessing. Manuel became their king, and all lived happily as true Christians in this life."

In my version, I have changed the brothers' route to their gifts, and have added the apple groves at the end. It seemed fitting, given the fact that the healing power comes from an apple.

My editor has asked me, why an apple? I honestly don't know. Why not a pomegranate or a peach? The original story said "apple," and I kept it that way. Because the apple has so often—since the earliest translations of the Bible—taken the rap for sin among humans, I like the idea that it can bring life as well.

"THE FALSE KNIGHT ON THE ROAD"

One of the oldest of the English ballads collected by Sir Francis James Child in the 1880s, in his great multivolume tome *The English and Scottish Popular Ballads,* this is "The False Knight on the Road" number 3.

'O whare are ye gaun?'
Quo the fause knicht upon the road:
'I'm gaun to scule,'
Quo the wee boy, and still he stude . . .

is one of the Scottish versions. However, there are few variants of this particular story. Some made their way to America with Scotch-Irish immigrants, who mainly settled in Virginia and New England. Early printed versions in America were in *The Only True Mother Goose Melodies* and *The American Songster.*

The idea of the ballad, Child explains, is "that the devil will carry off the wee boy if he can nonplus him . . . but . . . the boy always gets the last word."

In fact, stories in which a fiend/devil/demon is thwarted by a smart answer are quite common in folklore.

As I was working on the story, it became clear to me that for modern sensibilities, the boy is in serious trouble—not from a devil, but from a stranger—"stranger danger," as we call it these days. So thinking about John Gacy, a modern-day mass murderer who worked sometimes as a clown at children's parties, I wrote this quasi horror-story version. As a grandmother and a grandaunt, too, I was glad to help the boy escape.

"HIRED HANDS"

This tale from Afghanistan can be found in both Eric and Nancy Protter's *Folk and Fairy Tales of Far-off Lands* and Joanna Cole's *Best-Loved Folktales of the World,* where it is known as "The Farmer and His Hired Help."

Squarely in the trickster category of tales, where an underdog fools the wicked or stupid master, the story is a popular one in Afghanistan. However, trickster stories are found in every country and every folk culture of the world.

This particular story is both a trickster story and a teaching tale, for it explores the world of master and serf. The Protter and Cole versions are clearly modern reworkings—the youngest brother tries to shoot the cuckoo with a gun, and the ending reads as if the story had been used in a Communist government tract:

Never again did [the farmer] trick hired hands into unfair contracts, but on the contrary he began to offer better working conditions. He noticed with surprise that a lot more work got done when his men were happy because they were well treated.

I have given the boys Afghan names, and I have added Abdullah buying out the contracts of all the other farmhands, because though it is never stated in the Protter and

Cole versions of the tale, surely the other men working the fields had been tricked, too. In true fairy-tale fashion, the good and smart younger brother, Abdullah, would have made certain that no one was left to slave without pay for the wicked farmer.

"MIGHTY MIKKO"

This is a fox version of "Puss in Boots" from Finland. Probably the most famous of the animal-helper stories, its best-known version was published in Charles Perrault's fairy-tale collection in the seventeenth century as "The Master Cat; or, Puss in Boots." Classified as tale type 545B (the *B* indicates the animal in the tale is male; *A*, female), the Perrault story was not the first literary version. An earlier variant, in which the cat was female, was printed in Straparola's sixteenth-century collection.

The Perrault version, though, is the one that took hold and was reprinted and spread, as Jack Zipes says, "through literary and oral versions that circulated during that time and later." The story has been collected all over Europe and the Mediterranean, across Siberia, as well as in India and the Philippines. Heidi Anne Heiner explains in her fairy-tale Web pages, "It also traveled with colonists and travelers from Europe to Africa and the American Indians."

The cat, of course, is not the only kind of helper in the many versions of this tale, though it is the most popular in Germany, France, England, and Scandinavia. In a number of variants, jackals act the cat part, or fairies, dead people, or trees. But second-most popular to the cat is the fox. An Italian version of the story, "Giovannuzza the Fox," is found in Italo Calvino's *Italian Folktales,* and an Armenian version, "The Miller and the Fox," is found in Susie Hoogasian Villa's *100 Armenian Tales.* According to Atelia Clarkson and Gilbert B. Cross in *World Folktales,* the helper in Greek, Russian, and Eastern European tales also is regularly a fox.

I have used the plot of Parker Fillmore's Finlandic version—which is little more than "Puss in Boots" with a fox instead of a cat and a dragon instead of an ogre—but shortened it considerably, and have written in my own scenes and dialogue. I have added some Finnish names and historical references as well.

Bibliography

"THE MAGIC BROCADE"

Cole, Joanna, comp. *Best-Loved Folktales of the World*. Garden City, New York: Doubleday, 1983.

Heyer, Marilee. *The Weaving of a Dream: A Chinese Folktale*. New York: Viking Kestrel, 1986.

Shepard, Aaron. *The Magic Brocade: A Tale of China*. New York: Pan Asian Publications, 2000.

"THE YOUNG MAN PROTECTED BY THE RIVER"

Chatelain, Héli, ed. *Folk-Tales of Angola: Fifty Tales, with Ki-mbundu Text, Literal English Translation, Introduction, and Notes*. Boston: American Folk-lore Society by Houghton, Mifflin and Company, 1894.

Encyclopedia Britannica, s.v. "Angola." 1967.

"THE DEVIL WITH THE THREE GOLDEN HAIRS"

The Complete Grimm's Fairy Tales. Introduction by Padraic Colum. Commentary by Joseph Campbell. New York: Pantheon Books, 1944.

Grimms' Tales for Young and Old: The Complete Stories. Translated by Ralph Manheim. Garden City, New York: Doubleday, 1977.

Thompson, Stith. *The Folktale*. Berkeley, California: University of California Press, 1977.

Yolen, Jane, ed. *Favorite Folktales from Around the World*. New York: Pantheon Books, 1986.

"EATING WITH TROLLS"

Asbjørnsen, Peter Christen, and Jørgen Moe, comps. *Norwegian Folk Tales*. New York: Pantheon Books, 1960.

Cole, Joanna, comp. *Best-Loved Folktales of the World*. Garden City, New York: Doubleday, 1983.

Emrich, Duncan. *Folklore on the American Land*. Boston: Little, Brown, 1972.

Thompson, Stith. *The Folktale*. Berkeley, California: University of California Press, 1977.

"KNEE-HIGH MAN"

Abrahams, Roger D., ed. *Afro-American Folktales: Stories from Black Traditions in the New World*. New York: Pantheon Books, 1985.

Carmer, Carl. *Stars Fell on Alabama*. New York: Farrar and Rinehart, Inc., 1934.

Courlander, Harold, comp. *A Treasury of Afro-American Folklore: The Oral Literature, Traditions, Recollections, Legends, Tales, Songs, Religious Beliefs, Customs, Sayings, and Humor of Peoples of African Descent in the Americas*. New York: Crown Publishers, 1976.

Hughes, Langston, and Arna Bontemps, eds. *The Book of Negro Folklore*. New York: Dodd, Mead, 1958.

"LANGUAGE OF THE BIRDS"

Afanas'ev, A. N. *Russian Folk-Tales*. Introduction and notes by Leonard A. Magnus. New York: E. P. Dutton, 1915.

Montejo, Victor. *The Bird Who Cleans the World and Other Mayan Fables*. Translated by Wallace Kaufman. Willimantic, Connecticut: Curbstone Press, 1991.

Thompson, Stith. *The Folktale*. Berkeley, California: University of California Press, 1977.

"THICK-HEAD"

Calloway, Colin G. *The Abenaki*. New York: Chelsea House Publishers, 1989.

de Wit, Dorothy, ed. *The Talking Stone: An Anthology of Native American Tales and Legends*. New York: Greenwillow Books, 1979.

MacMillan, Cyrus. *Canadian Wonder Tales*. London: Bodley Head, 1974.

"THE FISHERMAN AND THE CHAMBERLAIN"

Cole, Joanna, comp. *Best-Loved Folktales of the World*. Garden City, New York: Doubleday, 1983.

Htin Aung, Maung, and Helen G. Trager. *A Kingdom Lost for a Drop of Honey, and Other Burmese Folktales*. New York: Parents' Magazine Press, 1968.

Ledgard, Edna. *The Snake Prince and Other Stories: Burmese Folk Tales.* Northampton, Massachusetts: Interlink Books, 2000.

Thompson, Stith. *The Folktale.* Berkeley, California: University of California Press, 1977.

"JACK AND HIS COMPANIONS"

Jacobs, Joseph. *Celtic Fairy Tales.* London: David Nutt, 1892.

Kennedy, Patrick. *Legendary Fictions of the Irish Celts.* London: Macmillan and Co., 1866.

Thompson, Stith. *The Folktale.* Berkeley, California: University of California Press, 1977.

"THE TRUTHFUL SHEPHERD"

Dégh, Linda, ed. *Folktales of Hungary.* Translated by Judit Halász. Chicago: University of Chicago Press, 1965.

Hargitai, Peter. *Magyar Tales.* Amherst, Massachusetts: University of Massachusetts International Studies Program, 1989.

"AND WHO CURED THE PRINCESS?"

Cole, Joanna, comp. *Best-Loved Folktales of the World.* Garden City, New York: Doubleday, 1983.

Noy, Dov, ed. *Folktales of Israel.* Translated by Gene Baharav. Chicago: University of Chicago Press, 1963.

Parsons, Elsie Worthington Clews, ed. *Folk-lore of the Sea Islands, South Carolina.* Cambridge, Massachusetts, and New York: American Folk-lore Society, 1923; Chicago: Afro-Am Press, 1969.

Thompson, Stith. *The Folktale.* Berkeley, California: University of California Press, 1977.

Zipes, Jack. *The Great Fairy Tale Tradition: From Straparola and Basile to the Brothers Grimm.* New York: W. W. Norton, 2001.

"THE FALSE KNIGHT ON THE ROAD"

Child, Francis James, ed. *The English and Scottish Popular Ballads.* New York: Dover Publications, 1965.

Crossley-Holland, Kevin. *British Folk Tales: New Versions.* New York: Orchard Books, 1987.

Flanders, Helen Hartness, ed. *Ancient Ballads Traditionally Sung in New England,* vol. 1. Philadelphia: University of Pennsylvania Press, 1960.

"HIRED HANDS"

Cole, Joanna, comp. *Best-Loved Folktales of the World.* Garden City, New York: Doubleday, 1983.

Leach, Maria, et al., eds. *Funk & Wagnalls Standard Dictionary of Folklore, Mythology, and Legend.* New York: Funk & Wagnalls, 1972.

Protter, Eric and Nancy, eds. *Folk and Fairy Tales of Far-off Lands.* Translated by Robert Egan. New York: Duell, Sloan and Pearce, 1965.

Thompson, Stith. *The Folktale.* Berkeley, California: University of California Press, 1977.

"MIGHTY MIKKO"

Calvino, Italo. *Italian Folktales.* Translated by George Martin. New York: Pantheon Books, 1980.

Clarkson, Atelia, and Gilbert B. Cross, eds. *World Folktales.* New York: Charles Scribner's Sons, 1980.

Encyclopedia Britannica, s.v. "Finland." 1967.

Fillmore, Parker. *The Shepherd's Nosegay: Stories from Finland and Czechoslovakia.* New York: Harcourt Brace Jovanovich, Inc., 1922.

SurLaLune Fairy Tale Pages. Heidi Anne Heiner. www.surlalunefairytales.com/pussboots/index.html

Villa, Susie Hoogasian, ed. *100 Armenian Tales.* Detroit: Wayne State University Press, 1966.

Zipes, Jack. *The Great Fairy Tale Tradition: From Straparola and Basile to the Brothers Grimm.* New York: W. W. Norton, 2001.